A
HARLEQUIN
Book

PROMISE THE DOCTOR

(Original title: *Sister Benyon's Promise*)

by

MARJORIE NORRELL

HARLEQUIN BOOKS

Winnipeg • Canada   New York • New York

PROMISE THE DOCTOR

First published in 1966 by Mills & Boon Limited,
50 Grafton Way, Fitzroy Square, London, England,
under the title *Sister Benyon's Promise*.

Harlequin edition published September, 1966

*All the characters in this book have no existence outside the
imagination of the Author, and have no relation whatsoever to
anyone bearing the same name or names. They are not even
distantly inspired by any individual known or unknown to the
Author, and all the incidents are pure invention.*

CHAPTER I

'Joy!' Her sister's voice, from the couch in the small living-room downstairs, sent Joy Benyon hurrying through the rest of her toilet at breakneck speed. She was accustomed to hurrying these days, she thought with a smothered sigh, but with things as they were it seemed more like working on a busy casualty unit, with a fresh catastrophe coming in almost every half hour.

'What is it, love?' She was back downstairs, still fastening her freshly laundered apron over her crisp deep purple uniform. 'I haven't much time. . . .'

'You never have.' Lana's tone was dispirited, sounding utterly without hope. 'Nobody has any time for me these days. Mother's taken on that extra book-keeping. Pete's always studying, and so are the twins. Now you haven't time to get me anything different for my breakfast.'

'I'll do you something, dearie.' Cousin Emma, well past middle age and often in pain from the rheumatism which had grown steadily worse over the years, came quietly into the living room, her homely face creased in worry as she saw Joy's anxious glance at the clock. 'What would you like?'

'That's just it,' Lana announced. 'I can't think of anything interesting. I don't want any more cereals or eggs. You haven't time to stop and cook anything tempting. . . .'

'Now, now!' Emma approached the day couch and smiled down at the girl, wishing—as they all wished— there was something she could do to help, but—she stifled a sigh—Doctor Frankton had assured them all they and the hospital authorities had done all in their power to help Lana, that what was lacking was a belief in herself, will power to complete the work they had already done. 'You know quite well we're all working together to try and find the deposit for one of those little houses you said you liked on that new estate just outside

the town! We can't all be at home to look after you!
I only wish there was something I could do to help.'

'You're doing enough, Emma.' Joy smiled at the
older woman, adding brightly: 'There are some mushrooms I brought back with me last evening. We were
going to have them with grilled steak and tomatoes when
I came home tonight, but I can bring some more.'

'We won't want mushrooms twice in one day either,'
Lana began to protest, but Joy stooped and kissed the
lovely face, still the loveliest face she had ever seen
despite the marks of pain and, lately, of deep depression.

'We aren't all having mushrooms for breakfast, pet,'
she pointed out. 'We'll have ours later, just as we
planned, because Mum and the others will be looking
forward to them—they're amongst Mum's favourite foods
—and I'll try and find something else for you, if the
little shop on wheels which comes round to the hospital
has anything tempting, something I know you'll enjoy.'

'Sorry I'm such a misery,' Lana said penitently,
returning the kiss. 'It's just that I get so fed up with
everything.'

'I know, love.' Joy gave her a quick hug, thinking
of the gay and lively girl her sister had been just over
three years previously. Right until she had happened
the accident, riding as pillion passenger on a friend's
motor-scooter.

At the time of the accident Joy had not been at home.
She had been working as staff nurse in the big provincial
hospital where she had completed her training, but when
she heard that after six weeks in the Wilborough General,
Lana still could not walk, she had had herself transferred,
going as the youngest Sister on the staff to Wilborough
General where the shortage of nurses and Sisters was
acute. Lana had been from hospital to hospital, but
all with the same result. At each one she was told there
was no sign of permanent injury or organic disease.

Elderly Doctor Julian Frankton, who had brought all
the Benyon babies into the world, had spoken frankly to
Joy when she had first come home to see what she could
do to help.

6

'It's a form of hysterical reaction, Joy,' he had told her. 'You've had a certain amount of experience with varying neuroses, and this appears to be one of them. We can only help Lana if we can in some way completely resolve whatever conflict exists in her mind and is the cause of this . . . almost refusal to walk, to be independent again. We can only be patient, sympathetic and try to direct her energies into useful channels.'

Joy had thought a great deal about what the doctor had said. He was right in saying she had nursed other such cases, and she knew the main causes of what was known medically as 'hysterical reaction' were usually that the patient herself was using her illness to escape the responsibilities of her daily living, although this 'escapism' was totally unconscious.

'It's mainly because of Tony,' Joy had thought to herself at the time, and although she had never met him, mentally she was still certain this unknown young man was the cause of her sister's prolonged state of inactivity.

At the time when the accident happened, Lana had been fresh from modelling school and just beginning to become known in the circles where such jobs were found. Tony, so Joy's mother had written her, was a promising young photographer, and he and Lana had struck up what promised to be more than a friendship. They had been going around together for some months, when, for what reason neither Joy nor anyone else seemed to know, they had a quarrel, and Lana, against Tony's wishes, had gone for a ride with his friend.

At first Tony had come to the hospital fairly regularly, then, so gradually that in the beginning it had seemed quite natural, he had been 'busy' whenever visiting day came around. Now, although Lana had been home almost two years, he had called at the house only once, and then he had not stayed very long, saying that he had an appointment and that it was an important contact and he must not be late! Joy knew that, before the accident, Tony and Lana had talked of being married one day in the not too distant future, and now it seemed

7

that with Tony gone from her life, the impetus to help herself to recovery appeared to have vanished with him.

Joy had settled down to the routine of living at home —much to the disapproval of Matron who would never have countenanced such a thing had not the shortage of good nurses and Sisters been so acute. As it was, she kept a stern eye on Joy, daily, it seemed, watching for some point or other which would give weight to her point that 'it's too much for you to be Sister at the General and to help look after your sister at home.'

Matron was in her late fifties and prided herself upon being 'one of the old school'. She held a firm conviction that to be a nurse—a *good* nurse—one must be completely dedicated to the profession. She believed strongly in discipline, both in oneself and in the hospital itself, and expected the Sisters on her staff to live as she did, the Wilborough General being the focal point of her life.

' I still say it will not be long before you're finding the strain too much for you,' she had told Joy severely, and the girl had immediately protested.

' I don't think so, Matron.' She could remember her passionate avowal. 'I'm a strong person. I'm sure I can cope. It isn't that Lana will take much actual nursing.'

' I shall watch you most carefully for signs of strain or of undue fatigue,' Matron had told her stiffly, and Joy had felt herself almost dismissed before she began there.

' I feel I can do it,' she remembered saying, 'but if you think it will be too much for me, I'll try St Anthony's across the town. . . .'

' No need to do that!' Matron had told her promptly. 'We need good Sisters here, at the General. Providing you *can* carry on in this manner without allowing your work here or your health to suffer in any way, I will not object further.'

That had been all. But Joy knew Matron was always watching, always checking up and the girl knew she would be ' on the carpet ' in no uncertain manner, should she fail in any way whatsoever to come up to Matron's required high standard.

'Come on, Joy.' Pete Bradley, qualified as an accountant with a local firm and recently accepted as a junior member, ran downstairs to join them. 'I can give you a lift this morning, if you like. I'm going out on a call and it's not far from the General. It won't take a minute longer to run you right to the gates.'

'Thanks, Pete. Just let me get my things together.'

There *were* difficulties in living at home which she had not really thought about until she actually encountered them. She always took a spare apron and so forth with her—one never knew what might happen between Cranberry Terrace and the hill she always had to climb to reach the hospital! Now she snatched up the things she had already packed in her small daily case, took a last glance in her mirror and ran back to kiss Lana and Emma good morning.

'I like you being on this turn, Joy,' Lana said unexpectedly. 'I do seem to see a bit more of you than when you're on nights.'

'I like it better myself,' Joy confessed, wondering as she spoke if this was strictly true, for on nights, unless one happened to be on the maternity unit where Matron always seemed to find especial interest one ran less danger of encountering her all-seeing eye and consequent disapproval should anything have gone wrong. So far, touch wood, there had been little of which Matron *could* complain, and so far as lay in her power Joy was determined things should remain that way.

'Sorry to have held you up, Pete,' she apologized as she settled herself in his little green mini. 'Things were . . . just a bit out of hand this morning. The twins were excited about it being the last week of term, Mother was in a flap because Miss Wilkinson wanted to be off early on a long weekend. . . .'

'And Lana playing you and Emma up as she always does when there's any sort of scramble for either of you!' Pete returned quietly in a casual tone which seemed to take any especial meaning away from the words, unexpected though they were. As usual, Joy was up in immediate defence of Lana's irritable and awkward moods.

9

'She doesn't mean to be difficult,' she sighed. 'It must be dreadfully wearisome to lie all day on that couch with nothing much to do except to read or watch television or listen to Cousin Emma. Personally I could listen for hours to her stories of what things were like when she was young, but I can well imagine Lana gets a little tired sometimes. She was always so active, before this happened—Lana, I mean.'

'I know.' Pete halted for the traffic lights and went on talking, not looking at her, but he was aware in every fibre of his being of the slim figure beside him in the trim Sister's uniform, the colour of which did such delightful and unexpected things for her eyes and for the lights in her hair. It was not much use to say any of this to Joy, as he had already found out. She was only too conscious that beside Lana, with her hair of fine spun gold, her rose-petal skin and wide eyes of baby blue with their unexpected fringe of long, tangled lashes, she looked almost colourless. She did not, Pete thought to himself, realize that the purple of her uniform brought out hidden depths in her own eyes of a darker blue than Lana's, and that by the same means unexpected lights in the hair she dismissed airily as 'just plain blonde'. In Pete's opinion there was nothing in the least 'just plain' about Sister Benyon, except her plain common sense, and sometimes that could be just a little too wearing, since she never appeared to count the cost of her devotion to her sister, or realize just how much of her own life she was giving up on Lana's behalf.

'I brought Lana one of those do-it-yourself jewellery-making outfits yesterday,' he said now as their line of traffic moved forward and he put out the indicator ready to turn left and up the hill. 'She wasn't interested. Maybe if we could find something which would occupy her mind as well as her hands . . . I know your mother tried her with some copy typing, but she said it was too difficult to cope with the machine on the bed-table, but I don't think she was interested enough to try,' he ended candidly.

'That's just it.' They had reached the top of the hill

and were turning into the side road which led to the General. 'She simply isn't interested in anything or anybody, not any longer. It frightens me sometimes.'

'Don't worry so much,' Pete advised, stopping the car at the entrance to the hospital used by the staff only. 'It's too much for you, and for your mother. Thank goodness I've finished my training now and it won't be long before I'm in a better position, then I can do a little more towards helping.'

'You do help, Pete.' Joy smiled at him, meaning every word, as she banged the door of the little car shut and turned to leave him. 'I don't know how we'd have managed without you all this time.'

'The boot's on the other foot, Joy.' Pete was serious. 'I shall never cease to be grateful to you and your mother for all you've done.'

'Then we're all satisfied!' Joy glanced at her watch and knew she'd have to hurry now. 'See you tonight, Pete. And thanks for the lift. If you're back first tell Emma not to worry, I'll find something different for Lana's tea,' then she was off, walking with her quick, brisk step in the direction of the Women's Surgical Unit.

The courtyard was mercifully deserted as Joy thankfully sped across and to the Sisters' room to take off her cloak. She still had five minutes to spare, something she had not expected amid the chaos of home that morning. She was just slipping on her clean cuffs when young Nurse Abbot came hurrying in search of her.

'Glad you're on time this morning, Sister,' she began. 'We're having a little trouble with Mrs Histram . . . She's convinced she's going to die, and heaven knows what we'll have on our hands before she's left us! I don't like hysterical patients. I was once on a ward where it started just in the same way with only one woman, and before we knew where we were it had gone like wildfire, half round the ward.'

'I know what you mean,' Joy sighed. She knew only too well. 'Hysteria's as contagious as measles! How about the hysterectomy?'

'Mrs Barker? Good as gold and trying her best not to be any trouble. Wish every patient took her common-sense views about what we're trying to do for them.'

'Most of them do,' Joy returned. 'Mrs Histram is an exception, but one can understand. . . .'

They went on into the ward, from the depths of which Joy could hear the sound of muffled, hysterical sobbing and the brisk tones of Staff Nurse Wilson's calming response, given in her most soothing and professional tones. She felt suddenly sorry for plump, comfortable Mrs Histram. She had come into the General two days ago for a simple curettage, with no trouble whatsoever anticipated, but she had arrived in a state of high nervous tension which had, it seemed, increased hour by hour. She was in her late middle years and had never before been inside a hospital, and what she had read and imagined had built up in her mind to a state of absolute fear, a condition which would have to be dealt with medically, by the R.M.O.'s prescribing a sedative or by some other calm-inducing means. At the moment, Joy could only feel sorry for the woman and her unreasoning fears, knowing that it was a similar state of mental stress which made her own sister's such a difficult case to deal with and to nurse.

She went quietly into the ward. Mrs Histram was sobbing quietly now, but Joy knew the effect this was likely to have on the rest of her patients. She walked over to the woman's bed, but as she was about to speak a deep voice sounded behind her.

'Good morning, Sister. I've written up a sedative for Mrs Histram. I don't think you'll have any further trouble with her this morning. We've had quite a friendly little chat, and she's feeling much better about things already, aren't you?' he asked the question, confident of the reply.

Mrs Histram did not disappoint him. Doctor Mark Stanton, R.M.O. of Wilborough General, was not an easy man to disappoint!

'Yes, Doctor. Thank you,' she said in a small voice which to the trained ears about her still held the strain of repressed emotion, of fear held, for the moment, completely under control.

'That's fine.' He patted her hand gently as he moved away. 'We'll have another little chat when you're feeling better,' he told her. 'I know you'll agree with me you're going to feel fine in a very little while, and you'll wonder why you didn't come in sooner!' He signed to Nurse Talbot to administer the prescribed sedative, then, speaking softly to Joy, proceeded with their tour of the ward.

There wasn't anything else of a particularly alarming or worrying nature, and by the time Mark had left, Joy was feeling more herself—her usual capable self—the self she normally felt on duty, and less the bewildered and worried sister she had been earlier that morning. Why was it, she wondered as she turned to her desk and looked over the report sheets, it was always so much more difficult to nurse a member of one's own family than a ward full of strangers, all with varying degrees of varying illnesses and post-operative or ante-operative conditions? There was no answer to the question she was asking herself, and as little Nurse Bagshaw began to push round the breakfast trolley, Joy forced herself to put all her home worries into the background of her mind and to concentrate on the task in hand.

CHAPTER II

The work on the ward went smoothly enough as Mrs Histram gradually calmed down and became quiet. The remainder of the patients in the ward appeared to be, in some cases, equally gradual in their process of awakening. Some of them, as a few always were, seemed quite lively, others were not, as yet, quite so interested in all that was going on around them, but all were pleased by the Sister's and the nurses' obvious interest in their wellbeing, all of them responding in their varying ways, so that, as always, Joy felt that satisfying sense of contentment, fulfilment, in her chosen work as her day settled to a customary routine.

There were three new admissions into her ward that morning. A Miss Paling, a slight, frail and elderly spinster who reminded Joy instantly of another such patient she had nursed in this self-same ward some months ago. Little Miss Paling had been admitted with almost the identical form of heart trouble which had finally cost Miss Barnes her life. Joy turned away, after making certain her new patient was as comfortable as she could be, an ache in her heart as she read, without a word being spoken, the same story of loneliness and seclusion which had been written all over Miss Barnes' face, until she had made a friend and confidant of Sister Joy Benyon.

The other two were much younger than the little spinster. Mrs Bredon was a cheerful young matron who told Nurse Talbot in a shrill voice, which at Staff's repressive glance she tried hard to tone down and failed, all about her ' Timmy and the three bouncers ', as she referred to her husband and, apparently, her three young children. All, it appeared, were full of such exuberance and the joys of living one could almost imagine Mrs Bredon was almost looking forward to the rest which would follow the thyroidectomy for which she had been admitted.

'Mrs Bredon should have been in Women's Medical for her pre-operative treatment, Sister,' Staff remarked, studying the patients' bed card, 'but they're full to overflowing. Matron has had them put three beds in the emergency side ward, and you know she doesn't like doing that unless she's absolutely compelled to.'

Mrs Bredon was settled quickly and happily and was soon chatting eagerly to her left-hand neighbour. The condition of her hair and skin, and her excess weight, all symptoms of her complaint, did not appear to be worrying her in the least, as with so many patients who had been admitted in like condition. Joy made a mental note to have a quiet word with Mark Stanton when he made his next round, or with the young house doctor, Philip Steadman, but newly arrived at the General. She turned away still wondering what Mrs Bredon had dosed herself with to produce such a lighthearted top-of-the-world condition so unusual in someone in her state of health.

By the time Matron paid her normal morning visit to the ward, everything was under control. As she spoke with her usual crisp but courteous diction to Joy and to the staff nurse, the girl breathed a sigh of relief. It was not until then she allowed herself to realize just how much she had been hoping her late arrival—or near-late arrival—that morning had been passed unnoticed.

The mid-morning drinks trolley was on its way round the ward when a student nurse from one of the medical wards came quickly to where Joy was sitting, writing at her desk.

'Matron says will you please come along to her office at once, Sister Benyon,' she announced. 'She asked me to say will you please not delay?'

'Very well. Thank you.' Joy blotted the page, screwed the cap back on to her pen and rose, casting a quick, all-seeing glance round her ward. Everything appeared in order. Even Mrs Histram was now dozing peacefully. There could not have been anything wrong which had attracted Matron's attention as she made her round, at least nothing to which she would not have made reference on the spot! No, Joy concluded with an inward sigh, whatever it was it must be applicable to herself alone! There was nothing to be gained by idle speculation, however, and Matron had specified that she wanted Joy there as quickly as possible, but as she walked briskly though sedately as became her position, along the corridor and down the stairs and along to Matron's office on the ground floor, she searched her mind for possible causes for this summons to Matron's office at this hour of a busy morning.

She could not think of a single thing for which she could be held responsible and which, in some way, although in what way she could not at the moment imagine, had offended Matron's ideas as to what was right and proper in the conduct of one of the Sisters at the Wilborough General.

There was only one other thought in her mind. It was the thought that something disastrous might have happened to someone she held dear, to her mother, Lana or Cousin Emma or one of the twins, or even to Pete who had driven her to the hospital that morning.

It was fifteen years since an accident had robbed the little family of their father. Joy had been very young, but old enough to receive the impact of the shock which had left Aileen Benyon with two little girls at school age and the twins still babies to support and to bring up alone. It had been the same accident, a coach returning from London on icy wintry roads which had crashed badly, and which had robbed the youthful Pete Bradley of both parents at the same time. In spite of her own grief, Aileen Benyon had offered the boy a home with herself and her small family, just as soon as she learned he had no other relatives of his own. Pete had been with them ever since, sharing their sorrows as he had since then shared their joys.

Now, with Aileen out all day, working, Joy knew, far too hard and hurrying and scurrying about in her efforts to make certain elderly Cousin Emma was not over-worked, Joy felt again that dreadful fear which always swept over her whenever she heard of any accident or disaster, staying with her, however busily her hands were employed, until she was assured that the little family circle was still intact.

She tapped lightly on the door of the office and in response to Matron's brisk invitation to enter, opened the door. Matron was seated at her desk, an elderly, reassuring gentleman facing her, a gentleman who rose at Joy's entrance and who was promptly introduced to her as 'Mr Belding, a solicitor from Vanmouth'.

Matron motioned Joy to be seated and, primly erect at her desk, began to speak.

'Do you recall a patient by the name of Barnes, Sister Benyon? A Miss Muriel Barnes?'

'Very well.' Joy had a swift mental vision of the sweet-faced old lady she had grown to love so well. It was always a mistake to allow one's personal emotions to become too involved where a patient was concerned, Joy knew. But there had been something 'different' where little Miss Barnes was concerned. She had been so quiet, so anxious not to give any trouble, so meticulous in her personal habits and so considerate towards everyone else, that she had woven her way into Joy's young heart.

'I am Miss Barnes'—that is to say the late Miss Barnes'—solicitor,' Mr Belding informed her as Matron paused. 'My firm has looked after the Barnes family's interests for a matter of three generations.'

Joy made no comment, but Matron, who appeared to feel that this whole thing was wasting valuable time for one of her nursing Sisters as well as for herself, took up the story.

'It appears that the late Miss Barnes has made you sole inheritor of what she had to leave, Sister,' she said crisply. 'Mr Belding could not find your private address in any of Miss Barnes' papers, and he could only contact you through the hospital. That is why he is here this morning.'

'Miss Muriel was the youngest of three sisters, Sister Benyon,' Mr Belding told her. 'She was also the last remaining member of her family. She has left you her house and its contents—a place named Fernbank, standing in a very nice garden of an appreciable size—and a letter, the contents of which I beg you to note most carefully, for she told me she was " entrusting Sister with her dearest possession " and although she has made no legal provisos as to what you do with your inheritance, I feel I must say that I personally hope you will respect her last wishes.'

' Of course I will,' Joy said, without in the least wondering what those last wishes might be. ' I . . . just don't know what to say. . . .'

' Then Mr Belding had better hand the letter over to you, Sister, and allow you to get back to your ward,' Matron said briefly, her small smile touching the corners of her mouth for a moment.

' And I would like your present address, Sister Benyon, if you will be so kind!' Mr Belding was not going to be hurried unduly. He had a certain task to perform and he intended to carry it through.

' Of course.'

Joy looked round for something on which to write the required address, but Mr Belding already had his notebook and pen ready. With a smile in response to his own friendly one, Joy told him the address and what times she would be home during the next few days, and with a sigh of satisfaction he held out an envelope which seemed to be packed by pages of a letter, packed so that the envelope flap seemed in danger of bursting open.

' Miss Barnes talked to me quite a number of times before she was admitted to hospital,' Mr Belding said. ' If she had not been staying in Wilborough when she became so very ill I should have been able to visit her in hospital too, but as it was,' he spread his hands in a gesture of despair, ' we have been overwhelmed with work at the office and my time has been fully occupied for a very long time. However, my dear,' he went on, his tone as brisk as Matron's own, and with an apparently sublime unconcern as to the fact that he might be in any way interfering with the cause of duty for someone else, ' I do know she had various good causes very much at heart. Not, you must understand, in the form of special charities and so forth, but she took her responsibilities very seriously indeed, and it is these I feel almost certain she is handing on to you. Our articled clerk came here to see her on one occasion, I understand, and he said she pointed you out to him and said she was going to entrust you with the care of her "dearest possession". That could refer to a number of things, but I do know she was dedicated to the cause of preserving the beauty and selectivity of Vanmouth.'

'I see.' With Matron on the other side of her desk obviously disapproving of this intrusion into hospital routine, Joy felt this was as much comment as she ought to make at this point. Impulsively she made a suggestion, not certain whether or not her mother would approve, but it was too late to think about that now. 'Would you care to go to my home in Wilborough and have a meal with us, Mr Belding?' she asked. 'I come off duty at half past four, and it takes me about half an hour to get home, but my sister and cousin are there and would make you very welcome, should you arrive before I do.'

'That is most kind of you, thank you.' Mr Belding beamed on Joy and on Matron alike. 'Is there any rule about my calling for you as you come off duty?' he turned enquiringly in Matron's direction. 'We could travel together. I assure you I have been driving for nearly thirty years and so far have a completely clear licence! That would allow me to complete my business in this part of the town and we could talk on the way. There may be little points you wish to ask about. . . .'

'There's no rule against your calling,' Joy assured him, 'and I shan't keep you waiting.'

There was little more. Matron was obviously anxious that the meeting between Mr Belding and Sister Benyon should now be terminated as quickly as possible, and in a very short time Joy was on her way back to her ward, the letter seeming to be burning a hole in the pocket of her apron.

She was met at the door of the ward by Staff Nurse

Wilson. Marcia Wilson was a good nurse, and since Joy had been at the General they had seen many a crisis through together.

'New admission,' she said briefly. 'Girl of eighteen. The usual story, I suppose, but she's taken an overdose in an effort to " forget " . . . she won't forget the results of having taken it at all,' she said crisply. 'Nurse Talbot's with her now. We've used the stomach pump and she's going to be all right, but she's not feeling any too good right now.'

'I'll take a look,' Joy said, and walked across to the far end of the room where the girl lay, moaning quietly. She did not even attempt to look up as Joy bent over her, and after looking at the bed card, checking with Nurse Talbot and making certain everything had been done or was being done to give the unfortunate girl relief, she went back to her desk.

Lunch time seemed hours away, and the letter in her pocket crackled tantalizingly every time she moved. Little Miss Paling caught her eye and signalled that she would like to speak to Sister. Joy went across to the elderly woman, suddenly remembering how, just after she had first been admitted, Miss Barnes had looked at her just as appealingly and in much the same way.

'Yes, dear?' she said in her usual kindly tone. 'Is there something I can do for you?'

'I don't suppose so, Sister.' Miss Paling sounded weary to the point of exhaustion. 'I just want to know what I'm doing here. This is a ward for surgical cases, isn't it? My own doctor said nothing about an operation to me . . .' She began to sound quite worried.

'And nobody has mentioned operating on you, Miss Paling,' Joy assured her gravely. 'The reason why you are in here is because the medical ward happens to be very full just at the moment. We're crowded too, but a number of patients will be leaving the women's medical tomorrow, I understand, and you'll probably be taken over there. I see you're here for observation,' she added gently.

'That's what I understood,' Miss Paling said fretfully.

'Now I'm not so sure. But if *you* are sure, Sister, would it be any trouble if I asked to be allowed to stay here with you? Whoever is observing me or whatever you call it can surely do it just as well with me lying here in your ward as the one I saw down the corridor, can't they?'

'We'll see,' Joy smiled again, moving away, 'but the beds in here will all be required for our new intake on Wednesday, you know. That's the official day for admission to surgical wards here, unless it happens to be an urgent case, an emergency of some sort.'

'Well, see what you can do, please, Sister. I'm funny in some ways, I know, but I sort of feel I can trust your face, and you can't say that about the face of everybody you meet, can you?'

'Not exactly.' She knew what the woman meant, and was glad she had inspired the confidence that it is the duty of all nurses to inspire in their patients, but there was every possibility that Miss Paling *would* be transferred, and she must do her best to make certain the little lady was not upset by the change. 'You'll like Sister Kelly, too,' she said confidently. 'She's a great friend of mine.'

'But I couldn't talk to her about Jackie,' Miss Paling persisted. 'She might not understand, and I feel sure that *you* would.'

'And I'm equally certain Sister Kelly would be just as understanding,' Joy told her soothingly. 'Tell me about Jackie, and I'll see if there's anything I can do.'

'Jackie's my companion,' Miss Paling's thin fingers were plucking nervously at the sheet over her too thin body. 'He's a Minah bird, and he's a darling. I've left him with a neighbour for the present, but they're going away very soon, I don't know quite when, and I'm worried about what's going to become of Jackie until I get home.'

'I'll have a word with the Almoner and get her to come and have a chat with you. I'm certain she'll be able to think of some means of coping with Jackie's welfare until you are able to take care of him yourself.'

'Thank you, Sister.' Miss Paling blinked away the ready tears of weakness and smiled up at her gratefully. 'You don't know just how much you've put my mind at rest. Jackie's a darling, but at a time like this he's quite a responsibility, you know. And I love him . . . so much you might think I'm crazy.'

'I don't think you're in the least crazy,' Joy assured her gravely. 'I think Jackie is a very lucky Minah bird to have such a thoughtful and understanding owner. Don't worry any more about him. You can take my word that Miss Stanningley, the Lady Almoner, will find some way of taking care of him for you.'

Leaving Miss Paling still saying how grateful she was and how much more settled she would be in herself once she knew Jackie was going to be all right, Joy went across to the young girl who had been brought in as the emergency appendix. With one thing and another there was absolutely no possibility of a quiet moment in which she could even open the flap of Miss Barnes' letter and gain just a hint as to what she might find herself having pledged to look after . . . whether it turned out to be another Minah bird, an aged parrot, a family of cats or whatever it was . . . but after her conversation with Miss Paling she had begun to feel a little bit apprehensive, and she knew her uneasiness would remain until the letter had been read.

CHAPTER III

'I should read it anyway.' Marcia had stepped into Sister's office for a moment. 'I couldn't bear to wait until the afternoon tea break. It's *hours* away yet!'

'Not really,' Joy smiled at her friend's enthusiasm, 'but I feel just the same way . . . only I keep remembering how annoyed Matron would be if she walked in and found me reading a private letter on duty.'

'I shouldn't worry about it, anyway.' Marcia gave the toss of her auburn curls which invariably did when any discussion of restrictions of any kind arose. 'There are nurses wanted everywhere, and I'm sure every hospital hasn't got someone at its head who swears by the rules laid down in the early days of nursing! Some Matrons nowadays are really quite human. Where my sister's doing her training, up in the West Riding of Yorkshire, they have a youngish Matron and she's absolutely marvellous at understanding how different things are today.'

'The basic rules remain the same,' Joy said firmly, although secretly she had to admit that their Matron *was* a bit of a martinet she would say nothing against her, whatever her private thoughts might be! 'I shall just have to contain my soul in patience until I'm in Mr Belding's car and on my way home. I wonder,' she mused aloud, 'if he'll mind stopping at the supermarket in Wigmore Street. I wanted some mushrooms in the first place. Now I think I'd better get some cooked chicken as well. . . .'

'If he's going to help to eat it, then he ought not to mind stopping to collect it!' Marcia observed reasonably enough. 'But I shouldn't splash too much, not until you know what your inheritance consists of. Somehow Miss Barnes doesn't remain in my memory as the sort of person to have won the pools and hoarded her ill-gotten gains for years without spending any of it!'

'No, she wasn't like that,' Joy agreed, a mental

picture of the late Miss Muriel Barnes clearly before her. 'She's more likely to have left me a whole load of responsibility of some sort or another. Somehow, since I've chatted with Miss Paling I'm beginning to worry as to exactly what she *did* mean when she referred to her "dearest possession". Could be any one of a thousand things.'

'Sister! Would you please come and take a look at Mrs Bredon?'

Nurse Bagshaw looked a little frightened and distressed and Joy rose at once.

'I'll be back in a moment, Staff,' she spoke over her shoulder, 'then we can finish going through those lists.'

There wasn't much time to spare, after all, during the afternoon. What had promised to be a fairly peaceful day was shattered by one event after another, and when at long last young Cadet Nurse Lenton brought in Joy's afternoon tea, she was only too happy to sit back and relax for those few minutes it would take to drink the welcome brew.

'I should open it now.' Marcia lifted her own cup and fixed an interested gaze on the bulge of the letter Joy still carried unopened. 'I honestly don't know how you can sit there so calmly, when for all you know you might have in your pocket the key to a lifetime of ease and leisure!'

'I hardly think so,' Joy laughed, but the temptation *was* great, there was no denying the truth of that statement. 'Well,' she said reluctantly, 'just a peep! By the look of the envelope it'll take me hours to get through all this. I ought to save it until this evening.'

'I'd be consumed with curiosity,' was Marcia's only comment, and with a half-stifled laugh at her own feelings of guilt, Joy took the letter into her hands and began to tear the thick, heavily gummed flap.

She was quite right in her assumption that there would be a great deal to read through, but as she scanned the first of the pages she gave a startled little gasp.

'What is it?' Marcia was agog with curiosity. 'Anything good?'

'Just a large house,' Joy said faintly, 'with, it seems, an equally large garden, with a view of the sea and the shore which, so Miss Barnes had written, can't be beaten anywhere along the coast. She's left me the house and grounds, the contents and sufficient money to attend to the upkeep, the rates and all that sort of thing. It's in the form of an annuity of five hundred pounds a year, and she says it will last until I can pass it on to someone else. There's an elderly couple who've looked after her house and garden, and who've cared for Miss Barnes and her sisters for as long as they can remember. She says her father promised them they'd have "shelter and care" to the end of their days, so whatever they're like they'll have to stay.'

'And what about the sisters?' Marcia asked quickly. 'Are they in a nursing home or something?'

'Dead,' Joy was still scanning the letter. 'It says here . . . "now that I am the last of the family", so they must be.'

'Very interesting, Sister Benyon, I agree.' Matron's cool tones brought Joy, scarlet-faced, to her feet, and she flung a quick look in Marcia's direction which the girl correctly interpreted as 'make yourself scarce', and which she needed no second instruction to obey.

'I was just scanning Miss Barnes's letter as I drank my tea,' she was beginning, but Matron cut in almost at once. 'There will be ample time for that later,' she said quietly, 'when you have left the hospital precincts. In the meantime, I suggest you take the letter to your wardrobe and lock it up, then it will not remain as a continual temptation to you, not being close at hand. There is just one other point.' She raised her hand as Joy was about to apologize. 'You were barely on time this morning, as I saw from my window. That is why I am, as you are well aware, strongly opposed to my nursing staff living out of the Nurses' Home. I realize quite well how difficult it must be for you always to get away in sufficient time to arrive at the hospital early, but I would like you, for the future, to make a little more concentrated effort to do so.'

She sailed majestically from the office, and Joy, her cheeks still burning, hurried to the Sisters' cloakroom to put away the offending epistle. Fortunately everything in the ward was in order, and having had a word with the patient she had come especially to see, Matron left, her face impassive as usual, but Joy felt angry with herself for yielding to Marcia's pleas to know the contents of the letter, when it had really been against her own better judgement.

'Was she *very* angry?' Marcia whispered half an hour or so later as they worked together establishing a blood transfusion for Mrs Potter, newly brought up from the theatre.

'Not more than I expected her to be,' Joy whispered back. 'She mentioned that she saw I was barely on time this morning, which is true, but I thought it had passed undetected. I know she doesn't like her staff living at home, but,' she could not help the sigh as she thought of the chaos there had been that morning, 'she simply doesn't understand how difficult things can be when there's a family to contend with and Cousin Emma isn't feeling so good.'

'Get another job,' Marcia advised briskly. 'I would. There are nurses wanted everywhere, and I don't suppose Vanmouth is any exception to the rule! All you have to do is to give a month's notice . . . and you'll have to do that, anyway, if you're going to live in this house Miss Barnes left you! Or move into the Nurses' Home and leave the family to fend for themselves by way of a change.'

'I suppose I shall,' Joy said slowly. 'I hadn't really got as far as thinking along those lines. It's all too new. I hadn't even thought about the fact there won't be any more quarter days for the rent, either. If we *do* move, that is. And there isn't much point in owning a house and having the rates paid for me if I don't live in it, *and* all the family as well. There are some good schools and what-have-you in Vanmouth, I think,' she began doubtfully. 'There's the problem of the twins completing their education. They're both bright as buttons, and I'd hate to do anything to upset things for them.

Then there's Pete. He's just beginning to earn himself something like a wage. He's been a long time on what was merely pocket money, you know. And there's Mother. She's always wanted something she could do at home . . . something in her own line, like a typing bureau or something. We've never been able to afford a room for her, and there certainly isn't even a vacant corner in the house at Cranberry Terrace.'

'You do meet your troubles halfway, I must say,' Marcia said meaningly. 'I shouldn't think about all that. I'd be off like a shot, and if the family know what's good for them they'll be along with you, you just see if they don't. Anyhow, it can't be like moving into the unknown. At least you'll have Miss Barnes' solicitor to advise you. I should take the plunge and hand in your notice. Vanmouth's a lovely place. A little select and choosy, but a very pleasant place to live in, I should think. It ought to work wonders for that sister of yours. One never knows. The prospect of being able to walk along firm, golden sand whenever she felt like it might produce the impetus to try again which she seems to have been lacking for so long.'

There wasn't time for any further conversation just then. In the usual manner of hospitals the world over, everything was geared to a timetable, a timetable which took emergencies and crises in its stride and expected the staff to be able to do the same thing. The remainder of the afternoon wore by at an amazing speed, but whenever she had a few seconds in which she could think of her own concerns, Joy found Marcia's words returning to her, until by the time she came off duty at half past four she had made up her mind that it would be foolish not to take the advice of the other girl.

Her heart seemed to be playing tricks as she tapped on Matron's door for the second time that afternoon. She need not have worried. Matron, having heard so much of what Mr Belding had said to her, was not in the least surprised when Joy asked to give her month's notice and said she would be leaving for Vanmouth as soon as was possible.

27

'I expected you to do this, Sister,' Matron sighed. 'I'm not in the least surprised, nor do I blame you. I have visited Vanmouth on more than one occasion, and found it a delightfully unspoiled resort. I suppose you will continue to nurse?'

'I hope so,' Joy agreed. 'I shall have to find out what hospitals there are in the area when I arrive.'

'There is the small St Lucy's at Vanmouth itself,' Matron surprised her by saying. 'And there is the larger General Hospital some miles out of the town. I should imagine it would be more convenient in your case if you could find employment at St Lucy's. And I will certainly do anything I can to help. I might also add,' she lifted her head and looked directly into Joy's eyes, 'that should you, at any time while I am still Matron here, wish to return to Wilborough General, we shall be delighted to have you with us again.'

'Thank you, Matron. That's very kind of you.' Joy felt her colour rising again and was annoyed with herself. Why should she blush simply because Matron had been surprisingly and unexpectedly pleasant and understanding?

'You are a good nursing Sister,' Matron commented, rising from the chair behind her desk, an action which Joy correctly read as being an indication that the interview was at an end. 'I have only one last word of advice,' she concluded. 'Beware that you don't always allow your heart to rule your head! It is not always a wise thing to do when one is a member of our profession!'

'I'll remember, Matron,' Joy promised, and even as she walked out of the hospital and across to where she saw Mr Belding sitting at the wheel of an enormous saloon car, she was still wondering if, all the time she had been on Matron's staff, she had been misjudging her when she had found herself full of resentment when she had been told off for just arriving on time, or for some little thing which might be held at her door because of her home circumstances.

'You look worried, Sister Benyon.' Jules Belding

28

made the observation as he drove down the hill from the hospital and, following her directions, joined the main stream of traffic at its foot. 'There isn't anything wrong, I hope?'

Mr Belding, probably by reason of his long association with the problems and worries of humanity in all phases and stages of life, seemed to invite confidences, and almost before she knew where she was Joy found herself telling him about how she had been 'on trial', as it were, ever since she had arrived at Wilborough General.

'I rather think Matron's bark is worse than her bite,' he observed, weaving his way through the tea-time traffic. 'Before you joined us this afternoon, she was full of praise for the way in which you conducted your ward, for almost everything about you.'

'Almost?' Joy pounced on the one word. 'What was wrong?'

'Just what she has said to you now, my dear.' Mr Belding halted at the traffic lights. 'You have a heart which, as Matron put it, would embrace the whole world, were it possible. That's the sort of thing which leads to a heart being broken if you're not very careful,' he warned. 'I'm not advising you to be hard or anything like that. You are the sort of person who couldn't be, anyhow. But do try now and then to think a little of yourself! Now,' he changed gear smartly and fell into line, 'tell me about this little family of yours into whose midst you intend to thrust me, a stranger. And by the way,' his shrewd grey eyes twinkled kindly, 'have you any shopping you wish to do on your way home? I know the arrival of unexpected guests always results in my wife telephoning local shops at the last minute, despite the fact that there is always a large, well-stocked fridge and cupboards full of whatever she's likely to need.'

'I did want to get something from the supermarket at the corner of Wigmore Street . . . just round the next bend, and it's the first shop on the corner of the junction, this side.'

'And I see we are allowed a parking time of twenty

minutes.' Mr Belding scanned the notice and switched off the engine, not two yards from the shop. ' Take your time,' he advised. ' Do you require any help?'

' No, thank you,' Joy assured him, but she was smiling to herself as she entered the supermarket and picked up her little wire basket at the door. He was rather a pet, she thought as she went quickly to the counter where the cooked meats were kept. If fulfilling whatever trust Miss Barnes had placed with her entailed the use of a solicitor, then she knew it would have to be Mr Belding and nobody else! There was something so reassuring and confident about him, he gave a strange reality to the fantasy in which she seemed to have been living ever since she had heard of Miss Barnes and her will and her letter.

Her purchases made, she came out of the supermarket to find Mr Belding engrossed in the day's copy of the *Financial Times*. He folded his paper as she settled herself beside him, squinting appreciatively at the transparent bag of fresh mushrooms.

' I hope you like them,' Joy ventured. ' Cousin Emma will never touch them. She's always afraid of being poisoned, and whenever we eat them she's always waiting anxiously for the first twenty-four hours to pass without incident, then she's certain we're all right.'

Mr Belding chuckled appreciatively, smiling with the understanding smile she had already come to associate with him.

' It's quite understandable,' he said tolerantly. ' Accidents *do* happen, I suppose. But they are very rare these days, and I should say the possibility is ruled out completely when one buys these cultivated mushrooms. It was quite a likely happening, however, in the days when one depended entirely upon those growing wild in the fields and picked and packed by people who did not always know a mushroom from a toadstool. Yes '—he finally got round to answering her question—' I like them very much. I look upon them as one of my favourite foods, but I'm sorry to say Mrs Belding doesn't always agree with me.'

Chatting of this and that, of food and their likes and dislikes, they finally arrived at Cranberry Terrace. Feeling suddenly shy of announcing that she was some sort of heiress, no matter of how small an inheritance, Joy ushered her visitor into the house.

Lana had recovered from her rather soured humour of the morning, and, as always, when anyone strange arrived, set herself out to be as pleasant and attractive as only Lana knew how to be. As Joy and Emma hurried about preparing the meal, Lana talked to the solicitor, and by the time a key in the front door announced the return of Aileen, the twins at her heels, Mr Belding was feeling almost like one of the family.

Everything was ready, the tea waiting in the teapot, when Pete, last always to return from his work of the day, came in, a look of surprise still on his good-natured young face as he pondered the large and impressive car outside their door. Introductions were quickly made, and Joy was grateful for the careful grounding in good manners which Aileen had given to each of her children. Everyone was obviously wondering why Joy had invited an unknown solicitor to share a meal with them, but everyone was too polite to ask questions. They were all waiting concealing their impatience as best they could, until she made her announcement.

No sooner had the creamed mushrooms and the cold chicken and fresh salad been served than Joy decided it was time to give them all a little idea of what had been happening.

'Mr Belding,' she announced gravely, 'has come to tell me that I've been left a house and garden, enough money to pay for its upkeep and some unknown special responsibilities . . . at Vanmouth. And this afternoon I gave in my notice at the Wilborough General. I only hope there'll be a place for me in one of the hospitals in or just outside Vanmouth!'

CHAPTER IV

There was a moment of complete silence as the family absorbed the unexpected and exciting news. Then it seemed that everyone's tongue began to wag at once, but as was their long-standing custom, as soon as Aileen began to speak the others lapsed into silence, leaving it for her to ask the questions trembling on their lips.

'Why?' Aileen asked first. 'And by whom, Joy? One of your ex-patients, I take it?'

'That's right. You remember I told you about Miss Barnes who was with us some months ago? She's left me her house in Vanmouth—Fernbank is its name— with a garden and an annuity of five hundred pounds, which will more than keep the place in repair, pay the rates and so on, and a few responsibilities which I'm not certain about at the moment but which will no doubt be explained in this letter'—she took it from her bag on the floor at her feet—'which Mr Belding brought to me at the hospital this afternoon.'

'Then perhaps Mr Belding will be kind enough to tell us a little about both the house, Vanmouth and Miss Barnes while you read your letter and learn your new responsibilities,' Aileen suggested, 'then we can begin to make plans.'

'It is by no means a new house,' Mr Belding began, 'but a very solidly built Victorian house with a conservatory and a garden which has always been well tended and cared for. The house has been modernized as much as old Mr Barnes thought it should be. That is, the electricity, plumbing and gas mains are sound enough and fairly new. There are three bathrooms. I think there are six bedrooms and four large airy rooms downstairs with a sizable kitchen as well. The interior decorations are not so modern as your own.' He glanced round appreciatively at the light paint and paper with which Aileen and Pete, with the help of the twins, had used throughout the house. 'But there is nothing else wrong with the place in any way at all. From the garden there is a good view down to the sea, but Mr Barnes had a high hedge built some years ago, and it is necessary to stand at the little gate in the hedge to get the view, unless,' he smiled, 'one is content to look through an upstairs window.' He cleared his throat gently and smiled at the silent, beautiful Lana. 'If I may say so, my dear,' he offered, 'the change of air, the new surroundings, might well work wonders where you are concerned. Vanmouth is a noted health resort, and with good reason.'

'What about schools?' That was Aileen, casting an anxious if loving glance at the twins. 'They should be sitting their G.C.E. examinations early in June.'

'There are some excellent schools in Vanmouth,' Mr Belding assured her gravely. 'As to the examination, that, I suppose, depends on whether they have been working on the same syllabus as the school to which they will, we presume, be changing. If I might make a suggestion, I should have a word with their present headmaster and ask him to get in touch with the examining board in question. I know the Vanmouth Technical College caters for about eight boards altogether, so maybe they would be sent there for the actual examinations when the time comes.' He turned to the twins, listening to his every word. 'Have you, either of you, any thoughts in mind as to the kinds of careers you wish to follow?'

'Well'—as usual, Sylvia left it to her brother to answer the question for them both—'I think I'm being a little too ambitious . . . for Mother's sake, I mean. What I want is . . . your line, Mr Belding, but it means a long time before I'm anything like independent!'

'It can be managed,' Mr Belding assured him gravely, 'if you are willing to work and remain interested in Law. We must have a chat together some time in the near future, and see what can be done. In the meantime,' his eyes twinkled, 'work on those G.C.E. examinations! They are of first importance, you know. And what about you, young lady?'

'She wants to teach,' Rex told him, giving a glance of brotherly amusement at his sister's small, intent face. 'She wants to teach infants and juniors . . . older ones might run her around too much!'

'I should imagine the boot might well be on the other foot,' Mr Belding observed. 'There is a great deal of patience required in the teaching of tiny children, I am sure, but both of you have worthwhile ambitions, and I'm certain, if you will do your share by working hard enough to pass the necessary examinations as they come along, we can quite look forward to each of you achieving your professional desires in the course of time.'

Unexpectedly he turned to Pete, not quite sure whether he was a relative or a friend. Whoever he was, Mr Belding had already decided, he was well enough known to the little family as to be looked upon as one of its members.

'And what about you, young man?' he invited Pete's confidence. 'Where do you fit into all this change?'

'I'm a . . . a friend,' Pete said slowly, as memories of just how good the friendship of the Benyon family had proved to be in his life. 'I . . . I've lived here for years. I expect I'll have to look round now for somewhere else to live . . . somewhere I can *afford* to live, until I get a little further up the ladder.'

'And your job?' Mr Belding asked, sounding, Pete decided, so really interested and friendly that he had none of his usual hesitation in confiding in this stranger.

'I've recently qualified as an accountant,' he explained, 'but although the firm I'm with have given me a position with them, I can't look forward to much advancement for a year at least.'

'I see.' Mr Belding eyed him for a moment, and sensed the bond which bound this young man to the family with whom he had lived for so much of his life. 'Would you be willing to enter industry?' he queried, 'in your own line, of course?'

'Yes,' Pete said promptly. 'I rather think I would like that.'

'Well, I can't, of course, promise anything, but I

think I may be able to help before the summer is through. Try and get yourself fixed up for the present time, and then we'll see what can be done.'

'Thank you, Mr Belding. Thank you very much.' Pete smiled, looking round at the others. 'I should hate to lose touch with the Benyons. They've been so very good to me.'

'There's no need to worry or to think we shan't always have a place for you, Pete,' Aileen said quickly. 'Mrs Parrott, just across the road, will be glad to look after you and she won't charge very much. What is worrying me'—her grey-blue eyes glanced round from face to face—'is how I'm going to help! If the house is so big, Cousin Emma won't be able to manage alone, and if I don't take some sort of job, even with the rent and the rates and so forth accounted for, it's going to be difficult for the youngsters to do what they want to do in the way of their careers . . . and I'd hate to disappoint them.'

'There's no need for anyone to be disappointed, Mother.' Joy looked up from the letter she had just finished reading, her eyes shining. 'Things couldn't be better for any of us,' she declared. 'Miss Barnes writes here about Mr and Mrs Wrenshaw, the couple who live in at Fernbank. Mr Wrenshaw looks after the garden and the outplaces, tends to the central heating and the open log fires Miss Barnes writes we'll find necessary in the winter months. He helps his wife with some of the household duties, is a general handyman and so forth, and Mrs Wrenshaw is, I quote from the letter, "a good cook and a capable housekeeper whose friend, a Miss Angel, always comes to help at spring-cleaning time and when there is anything extra to be done. If you can manage a little dusting or suchlike as an extra hand around the house",' Joy read on, still quoting from the letter, ' " you will be able to continue with your nursing, the career for which you have such a wonderful gift . . ." So,' Joy concluded, looking round as she folded up her letter, ' if Cousin Emma goes on as she is doing, and this Miss Angel comes when we need her,

35

there'll be nothing to stop you opening your own typing and what-not business as you've always wanted! You know you don't really like domestic chores, and this seems the ideal solution!'

'For everyone but *me*!' Lana said suddenly and sadly. 'This is going to be marvellous for everyone, but all it will mean to me will be to have this couch in another room, in another town, away from everything and everyone I know.'

'And a lovely garden in which to spend the coming summer,' Mr Belding said before anyone else could speak. 'The best of attention, as you are getting all the time, will still be there, but you'll have the added benefit of the sea air, the change of surroundings, and a new doctor who may have some suggestions to offer. At least,' he decided, 'you will not be any worse off for your move!'

There was no denying the wisdom of his words, and Lana lapsed into silence, knowing she was secretly as thrilled as the rest of them but that she felt so alone, so left out of things. Maybe Mr Belding was right, and as time passed she too might find some benefit from this unexpected change, but she would not allow herself to become enthusiastic. Ever since Tony had walked out of her life she had ceased to be enthusiastic about anything. She still followed his career through the newspapers, the career she had hoped to share. He had gone to London, and was already making a name for himself in the world of photography, but now he had other models, other girls in whom he was undoubtedly interested, and she suspected he had forgotten her very existence months ago.

'Well'—Mr Belding consulted his watch and rose, pushing back his chair—'I am afraid I really must be on my way. Thank you very much for your hospitality. I will leave the set of keys which belonged to Miss Barnes. Mr and Mrs Wrenshaw have their own, of course. Shall you be along to see your property before you remove, Miss Benyon?'

'I have half a day off next Thursday,' Joy told him,

'and that's Pete's half day too. Perhaps he'd drive me over?' She glanced at Pete, who nodded. 'So that's all right. There's just one point, Mr Belding. Miss Barnes says in her letter that Fernbank is what she meant by '' my dearest possession '' and that she trusts me to see to it that the house and grounds are not used in any way which will take away any of the select and beautiful aspects of the town she loved. Just what do you suppose she means by that? I do understand she took my promise to mean that, being trusted with the house, I would never sell it or anything like that, but it's this wording I can't quite understand.'

'A little while ago,' Mr Belding said gravely, 'some of the wealthiest of the town's businessmen decided to form a syndicate to provide us with a holiday village of bungalows, shops, entertainments and the like which most of the citizens would prefer to do without. I think Miss Barnes had reason to suspect they were more than a little interested in her house and the grounds, and the strip of ground which adjoins it and runs down to the road which leads to the sea. I know that before her sisters died they tried to purchase that particular piece of land, but the man who owns it was not interested in selling. He is a member of this group who want to form the syndicate.'

'If Miss Barnes didn't wish them to have the house and grounds then I shall make it my business to make certain her wishes are respected. You can be certain of that!' Joy told him.

'I'm so pleased.' Mr Belding nodded, well satisfied. 'I felt from the moment we met that Miss Barnes had made a good choice in entrusting her responsibilities and her property to you! I shall look forward to seeing you if you have time to call in at my office on Thursday, and if not '—he handed her a card—'perhaps you will contact me there before you are ready to move, and if there is any way in which I can assist you I shall be only too pleased to do so.'

He said goodbye, and the entire family accompanied Joy to the door to wave goodbye, the entire family with

37

the exception of Lana. They returned to the house, chattering together ' like a bunch of magpies ', as Cousin Emma put it, and if Lana and Pete were the most silent members of the little household, their silence was not commented upon, since the others were too full of discussion to notice very much.

There was so much to be done in the few days before the Thursday. Aileen felt very guilty about giving up the extra book-keeping she had undertaken only a month or so previously in an effort to make a little more money, but she had begun to look so tired that Joy was thankful for her mother's sake that this early rising and extra work in addition to her post as secretary to a firm in Wilborough would soon be a thing of the past.

There was the matter of the twins and their further education. Aileen went alone—as she had done so much for her family entirely alone—to see the headmaster of the co-educational High School where they had both attended since passing their examination from the junior school. Mr Appleby was kind and helpful, sending along a letter for the twins to take to their new school, explaining which examining board the twins were to take their forthcoming examinations, so that if their new school had not the same syllabus there would be no confusion when their new teachers helped them through their next and final term before the examination dates.

The rent of the house in Cranberry Terrace was paid to the end of the quarter, so there was no worry about that side of affairs. By the time she relaxed in the seat beside Pete on their way to Vanmouth, Joy felt life had already taken a more rapid and more interesting turn for all of them.

' I hope Mr Belding can find something for you in Vanmouth, Pete,' she said, once Wilborough was left behind and they were speeding through the green countryside, dappled with the thin April sunshine. ' It won't seem like home without you, it seems you've always been there.'

' I have, just about.' Pete frowned at the road. ' It won't seem right going across the road to Mrs Parrot's every evening, but she was very sweet about it when I went to see her. She remembers my folks very well, which is more than I do. It seems to me that I've always been with you and the others. It'll be like parting from a real family of my own, once you're all gone . . . especially you, Joy.'

'You must come and see us just as soon as we're settled in. And you'll be able to have your holidays at Vanmouth as well,' Joy said quickly. 'Oh, look over there! Isn't that a skylark? It seemed to come down from such a great height and straight to the ground.'

'It'll have a nest not far away.' Pete liked to study birds whenever they were in the country. 'They never land close enough for one to trace them as easily as all that, though.' He went on to talk at some length of the various means by which birds and other forms of wild life disguised the entrances to their homes as a protective measure, and for the time being his attention was diverted. Joy heaved a sigh of thankfulness. She loved Pete, but as an older brother. Until recently she had thought he felt the same way about her, but now she was not so sure, and she did not want any emotional complications in addition to the domestic changes into which they had all been plunged willy-nilly.

'When I fall in love,' she thought as the car engine hummed beneath the bonnet and the miles fell behind them, 'I'll know, I'm sure. I seem to know I'll feel . . . differently, right from the beginning. It won't be Pete or anyone I've known all my life. It'll be someone right out of the blue . . . but I know I'll feel differently about him, whoever he is, right from the beginning!'

CHAPTER V

Vanmouth, of which she had heard much but never visited, proved a delightful surprise to Joy. The town was larger than she had expected, the traffic brisk and busy. There were several important-looking modern blocks of flats and offices which contrasted strongly with other parts of the town where the buildings were somewhat older although in an excellent state of preservation. Every road and traffic island bore its banks of flowers, and the streets were wide and tree-shaded. Around the town itself were cliffs on three sides, with what looked like a veritable forest of trees sweeping down almost to the sea and golden shore which made the fourth side of the township.

'It's lovely,' Joy breathed as Pete slowed down to ask someone directions as to their route. 'I think we're going to like living here. I wonder where St Lucy's is? Matron said it was in Vanmouth itself, but she didn't say where.'

'I expect someone will be able to tell us.' Pete turned into a wide road and slowed down to ask further directions of a passer-by.

They had not much further to go. Ahead they could see the gleam and glitter of the sun-flecked sea, but the road curved more than once, with little side roads on either side, and, as Pete remarked as they turned again into a wide half crescent, the distance through the town and the distance of the shore to the nearest houses, must both be equally deceptive.

'Mr Belding said Fernbank stood alone, almost the last house in its road before the sea . . . no, *the* last house,' she corrected herself quickly, remembering about the piece of land beyond her future home which the Misses Barnes had tried in vain to purchase. 'Do you think we're on the right track, Pete?'

'Navigation correct, ma'am!' Pete swung the little car to a halt before a tall, old-fashioned pair of iron gates with the legend 'Fernbank' woven into the design as part of the decoration. 'I should say we're here.'

Joy descended from the mini suddenly feeling shy and just a little afraid. After all, whatever Mr and Mrs Wrenshaw proved to be as people it seemed she was in honour bound now to be responsible for their welfare, since that was how Miss Barnes had taken the promise she had made to 'look after my interests. . . .'

'And I will,' Joy vowed mentally, pulling herself together. 'I can't let Miss Barnes down now! Not after she's put so much trust in me!'

With Pete closely beside her she walked firmly along the well-kept path to the wide, highly polished front door and pressed the bell. Almost before it had stopped ringing, or so it seemed, the door was opened and a small, round woman, barely reaching to Joy's shoulder but with a healthy, rosy face beaming with welcome, stood there, holding the door wide open.

'Come in, please do!' she began at once, her voice crisp and firm and not in the least like Cousin Emma's often weary-sounding tones. 'You must be Sister Benyon?' She looked enquiringly at Joy and then back at Pete. 'Miss Barnes wrote to us about you, before she was too ill to write much at all, that is. She said you had the kindest and most compassionate face in the whole of her experience, and that a body only had to take a look at you to know their life would be as safe in your hands as it could be anywhere on this earth! And this will be your brother, will it? It ran in my mind that Miss Barnes wrote that he and your sister—one of them —were still at school, but it's months ago now, and I forget so many things these days!'

'That's one thing you haven't forgotten, Mrs Wrenshaw,' Joy smiled, her blushes at the unexpected words about herself from the old lady beginning to fade a little. 'My brother and his twin sister, Sylvia, are both still at school. This is a friend of ours who has lived with the family for a number of years, Pete Bradley,' she completed the introduction. 'We shall have to look around Vanmouth and try and find work for him here,' she ended in a teasing voice. 'It won't seem the same home without Pete around!'

She stopped abruptly, covered in confusion by the look in Pete's eyes, a look she had never intended to call forth where she and Pete were concerned. Hastily she plunged into talk of the house, details of the furnishings, wondering how much extra furniture the family would need to fill all these rooms, but Mrs Wrenshaw seemed to sense what was running through her mind.

'There's more furniture in these rooms than we know what to do with, Miss Benyon, and that's a fact,' she said after introducing her husband, a small, neatly built man with snow-white hair and a small, trim white beard, a pair of twinkling blue eyes and the straightest back Joy had ever seen outside a military parade.

'There's a sight more up in the attics, too,' he said now. 'Old Mr Barnes had a mania for auction sales. Never bought anything of great value once in his life, but always lived in the hope that one day he'd pick up what he called "a collector's piece" somewhere amongst the rest of it. Most of the stuff is stored up there, but I dare say a lot of it could be put to some good use. There's a little place in the town where there are two young men who love . . . converting things, I think they call it. They'll be full of ideas.'

'We can talk about that when Mother has looked round,' Joy said as Mrs Wrenshaw proudly presented them with a lavish tea, ready laid in the dining-room. 'At the moment I'm only anxious to change the paper on the walls and the paintwork. It will be a little depressing for Lana if she has to lie indoors very much if we leave it the way it is.'

'That's your invalid sister, Miss Benyon?' Mrs Wrenshaw refused to sit down with them, saying that she and her husband would prefer to have theirs in their own room at the back of the house, but she stayed there just the same, evidently anxious to give what advice and help she could.

'Yes,' Joy said gravely. 'She can't . . . doesn't walk, yet. We hope she will, given time. It was an accident . . . when she was much younger, just at the start of a promising career.'

'Miss Barnes wrote us all about it,' Mrs Wrenshaw told her. 'And when I knew what she'd done about the house, Miss Barnes, I mean, I said to Eric here' —she indicated her silent husband—'we can do the old gentleman's study over for the young lady. She can use it as her bedroom. It opens into the conservatory which opens into the garden. She could have the best of things indoors and out, that way.'

'What a lovely idea,' Joy enthused, and when they were taken to see the study and discovered that there was a small alcove in it which would just take a single bed, she was more enthusiastic than ever. 'We could take it in turns to sleep down here if Lana wanted us to,' she pointed out. 'It should be all very easy to arrange.'

Everything, it seemed, was 'all very easy to arrange', and by the time they had completed a full tour of the house, with the exception of the attics, gone round the garden which held full promise of the sunny days to come, and admired the bedding plants Eric Wrenshaw had already grown in the greenhouse ready to transplant, there was not much time left to them. Alice Wrenshaw said she 'wouldn't rest' until Miss Benyon had taken a look at the extensive stocks of linen, china and glassware, cutlery and all manner of such things with which the house appeared to be well packed.

'You'll be able to set your mother's mind at rest, Miss Benyon dear . . . or should I say Sister?' she asked. 'Tell her we have plenty of everything we need. There's no need for her to buy anything extra at all, and there's plenty of room for whatever you bring along from your own home as well.'

By the time they said goodbye to the Wrenshaws, knowing they had made two good and faithful friends, the April dusk was falling, and Pete, after an anxious glance at his watch, announced they must not waste any time on the way if they did not wish to alarm Mrs Benyon!

43

It was a little tricky, finding their way back along the winding road out of this quiet part of the town, but once on the wide main road they recognized, they settled down to enjoy their return journey. Ahead of them, under the modern street lighting, they saw a heavy lorry with a loaded trailer behind it. Just at the side of the lorry a boy riding an errand-boy's bicycle pedalled hard to keep abreast of the lorry, but as they drew out of the thirty-mile limit and into the forty-mile zone of the town, the lorry put on speed and went ahead.

What happened next was, from Joy's point of view, horrible, but something which also made her instantly thankful for a careful and thorough training which had taught her to be of some use in the world. Afterwards they heard the boy had seized on the idea of taking hold of the back of the lorry to give him a tow along the road, something he knew to be both unwise and dangerous, but they were facts he chose to ignore when he was tired. It was quickly evident that he had not seen the trailer behind the lorry, and almost before the automatic protest against what they expected to happen had reached Joy's lips, the trailer had caught the lad a heavy blow and sent him reeling from his machine and almost into the electric light standard at the side of the road.

Like Joy, Pete had guessed what would happen, and it was his quick thinking and almost instant action which saved the boy from being run over in addition to his existent injuries, by Pete's oncoming vehicle.

Joy was out of the car almost before it stopped and kneeling beside the boy as he lay at the edge of the road. Pete had signalled the lorry-driver with his lights, and the lorry was pulled up too, just a little way ahead.

Where the people came from she never realized, but suddenly the road which had appeared almost deserted was crammed by curious sightseeing people of all ages and types.

' I've sent my boy to telephone for the doctor,' a man told Joy as she lifted the boy's head into her lap. ' Is there anything else I can do, miss? You look as though you know what you're about.'

44

'I'm a trained nurse,' Joy told him briefly. 'Yes, there is something you can do. Pop across to one of those houses on the other side of the road and try and borrow a broom or something of that nature. And some long strips of linen or sheeting or anything that will make a strip long enough to tie the broom to his leg. He's fractured it.' She gave the brief explanation as the man hesitated. 'I want to put on a temporary splint, then he must be taken to hospital. Have you asked your boy to telephone for the ambulance as well?'

'I didn't think of that,' the man confessed, still somewhat shaken by what he had seen. 'I just thought of Doctor Moyser. . . .'

'Don't!' Joy spoke the one word sharply as a woman from the little crowd gathered round the boy moved forward to lift him.

'He's moaning,' the woman complained. 'And his ears are bleeding. I can see.'

'He very probably has a fractured skull,' Joy said crisply, 'and to move him when it isn't necessary is likely to do more harm than good. I hope '—she ended almost under her breath as she worked on the temporary splint under the watchful eyes of the crowd of onlookers —'your Doctor Moyser won't forget to telephone for the ambulance before he leaves wherever he is!'

'I couldn't help it,' the lorry-driver was protesting. 'I passed him, normal like. Next thing I know is this young man here signalling me with his lights, and when I get back it's to find this young shaver on his back in the gutter and his bike smashed to bits, and it looks likely I'll get the blame for it. Folks always think it's the driver . . . but it seems to me he didn't even *see* the trailer, never mind about waiting to see if it was clear behind me and that he *could* hang on. It tells them in the Highway Code not to do it.'

'You weren't to blame, old man,' Pete assured him gravely. 'We saw what happened.'

'And now let's take a look at the result.' A firm, young man's voice came from somewhere just above Joy's head. She looked up to see a charming, thin face

45

with curiously slanting eyes looking down into her own, and suddenly, as their glances met and locked, it seemed that an electric current had passed between them. Whether anyone else had observed anything different about the moment or not, Joy neither knew nor cared at that moment. She knew she was trembling suddenly, and quite without reason, and with an effort she pulled herself together to listen to the stranger's words.

' Let me introduce myself.' He was giving an expert eye to the now finished job of the temporary splint. ' My name is Quentin Moyser. My father and I are doctors in practice around these parts. If I may say so '—he smiled suddenly directly into Joy's eyes and the smile seemed to be especially for her and her alone—' you've made a splendid job of that, Miss. . . .'

' Benyon,' Joy finished for him. ' Sister Joy Benyon, of the General Infirmary, Wilborough . . . at least until the end of the month.'

Uneasily Pete moved forward, and there was just time for Joy to introduce the two men to each other before the ambulance halted beside them and the uniformed figures of the ambulance men jumped out and took charge of the boy. A policeman had appeared, it seemed from nowhere, and as he came on the scene the little crowd melted discreetly, returning back to wherever it had emerged from and melting into the night.

The policeman took statements from Joy and Pete as well as from the lorry-driver, and muttering dark words about youths who wanted ' everything easy, even if they know it to be wrong and dangerous ', he went on his way after saying a cheerful goodnight to the doctor, whom he appeared to know very well.

' Well!' Quentin Moyser dusted his hands on the seat of his grey trousers and smiled again. ' You're probably anxious to be on your way,' he began hesitantly, ' but after an experience like that I think you might feel a little better for some hot coffee or tea . . . what do you say? I live just up the road. If you would allow me . . .'

' You're very kind,' Pete began stiffly, ' but it *is* late,

46

and . . . someone will be getting anxious about Miss Benyon here.'

'Can you telephone whoever it is?' Quentin asked promptly. 'How far have you still to go?'

'To Wilborough,' Joy told him before Pete could utter the 'not very far' she could sense was trembling on his tongue.

'That's all of fifty miles!' Quentin took her arm purposefully, obviously aware that Pete would automatically follow without waiting further invitation. 'You *need* that drink, and you can telephone from our house. Mother will be delighted to help.'

'There isn't anyone at home we can telephone,' Pete was beginning to protest again, but Joy smiled, meeting Quentin's glance again and feeling once more that strange sense of 'belonging' she had felt even at the moment of first meeting him.

'Mr Anderson, at the end of Cranberry Terrace, lets us use his telephone if we want to,' she put in. 'He always says we can ring him too if there is any message we wish to have taken home. He's a free-lance journalist on the local paper,' she explained to Quentin. 'A very pleasant man, and often he's found typing jobs and so on for Mother. He's very friendly, and he doesn't go to bed very early, so I know we shouldn't be disturbing him unduly. And I know Mother won't rest until she's certain we are safe.'

'That settles it, then,' Quentin decided. 'Mr Anderson it is, and he can deliver the message to your mother. Will you follow me?' He turned to Pete, but there was not even a shadow of doubt in his voice as he spoke, and without turning his head he got into his own green Jaguar and flashed his lights, waiting for Pete to fall in behind with his own smaller vehicle.

Pete's jaw was set grimly as he obediently swung into line behind the doctor's car, but he made no comment, only answered in the briefest of monosyllables as Joy talked to him on the short journey up the road towards home. Their excursion ended as Quentin swung into a wide, gently curving driveway bordered by wallflowers

47

in full bloom, their scent rising and entering the car as they passed.

'Here we are.' Quentin halted outside the wide, white porch and went ahead of them into the house. 'Come in, please,' he invited, then they could hear his voice in a further part of the house calling for his mother.

'In the kitchen, dear,' Celia Moyser called gently. 'I've just put the kettle on, and there's coffee perking.'

Quentin advanced into the kitchen and closed the sound proofed door gently behind him, smiling at the bright-eyed, brown-haired woman who was his mother and, as he so often told her, his truest friend.

'We'll decide in a moment, Mother,' he told her. 'When we find out which our visitors prefer. She doesn't know it yet, and I don't know what obstacles there may be in the way—including a young man who's with her right now—but there's the girl in our lounge I intend to make my wife. You're always urging me to "settle down" . . . now come and see if you approve of my choice!'

CHAPTER VI

If Celia Moyser was surprised by her son's declaration there was no trace of any such emotion on her pleasant, smiling face as, a moment or so later, she followed him into the lounge. Joy, who was accustomed to assessing people as and when she met them, liked her at once. She seemed so tiny beside her tall, broad-shouldered son, and the way in which she whisked about, brewing the tea they all declared they would prefer in place of the coffee, bringing out a tray of biscuits and cakes, all obviously home-baked, reminded Joy, amusedly, of a bright, alert little robin.

' I suppose your father will be able to tell us something about the unfortunate young man when he comes in.' She was speaking in reply to Quentin's story of the accident to which he had been called and at which he had found Joy helping and herself and Pete as witnesses. ' He's still at the hospital,' she concluded.

Joy leaned slightly forward, acutely conscious of Quentin sitting opposite to her and watching her intently.

' Would that be St Lucy's or the General?' she asked.

' St Lucy's.' Quentin's attention was arrested now. Surely he wasn't going to be so lucky as to have this unknown girl suddenly thrust into the midst of his working life? ' The General is just out of the town,' he explained. ' St Lucy's isn't far away. You must have passed the entrance road on your way up.'

' Then it can't be very far from Fernbank?' Joy asked further. ' The house the late Miss Barnes lived in?'

' And all her family before her for a generation or two gone by. I believe it was built by her grandfather,' Mrs Moyser contributed. ' No, St Lucy's more or less overlooks Fernbank, in a manner of speaking. That is to say St Lucy's is at the top of the hill above the road where Fernbank stands, on what is known locally as " the shore road ". What made you ask?' she went on. ' Have you been visiting Mrs Wrenshaw?'

49

The question, Joy knew, was not one of idle curiosity. She had learned a great deal during her talks with the late Miss Barnes, and one thing she had learned had been the wonderfully closely knit community which made up the select residential section of Vanmouth.

' It all seemed to begin in the war years,' Miss Barnes had reminisced. ' Somehow, when the first evacuees came along, right through every alert, every raid, even in other parts of the country, we all tended to draw nearer together. It was as though we drew comfort and assurance from one another just by being together . . . not in those awful shelters, you understand. But by sort of banding together as a community, and, thank heaven, although that sort of thing is now looked upon as being a little old-fashioned and isn't in keeping with what I've seen of the modern world of today, a great deal of that spirit has been left with those families who grew up together at that time, and I, at any rate, am thankful for it. We're all *interested* in what happens to the rest of us, whether it be good or bad. If it's good then we like to rejoice along with the fortunate ones, and if it's bad . . . well, it's surprising what can be done to help even in the most hopelessly stricken cases, if only there's more than one person to cope.'

Now, remembering her old friend's words, Joy knew the question for what it was, merely a friendly interest, and she felt a sudden warm glow of pleasure as she replied. It had made her feel she was already accepted as one of the community.

' We have been visiting,' she said now, ' but only because Miss Barnes surprised me by leaving Fernbank and its contents to my care. I never expected any such thing . . .'

' Then you must be the Sister she wrote to Mrs Wrenshaw about,' Celia said, nodding as though satisfied by something. ' I never heard your name, my dear, but I know you made dear Muriel as happy as she possibly could be, so far away from everyone she knew and who knew her.'

' I . . . thought she was entirely alone in the world,'

Joy confessed. ' No one seemed to come and see her. There was one young man, I remember, one visiting afternoon, but that was all.'

' That would be young Mr Napier, Mr Belding's articled clerk, or rather one of them.' Celia nodded as though this explained everything. ' That was when Muriel had the will drafted out for her signature. We should have all gone to see her, but she had expressly said she didn't want anyone she loved to see her in what she called " the state of health to which I am now re-duced ", and so, of course, none of us went to see her, not even Mrs Wrenshaw, though she would have willingly walked there if she had not realized how upset Miss Muriel would be ! '

' That would be why you said " at least until the end of the month " when you told me who you were,' Quentin put in. ' I take it you intend to move into Fernbank, then?'

' All being well.' Joy's smile, Quentin decided. seemed to do strange things to the emotions which so far he had never suspected existed where he was concerned. ' There's an awful lot to do and to plan first, though.'

' If there is anything I or my family can do to help at this end of affairs, you have only to say so,' Celia offered. ' I know just how difficult it can be to cope with hospital routine and attend to one's private affairs if they don't happen to be on the doorstep. Are you,' she asked so casually that again Joy knew there was no curiosity as such in the question, merely a friendly interest, ' a large family?'

' Not really. There's Mother. She's the prop and mainstay of the household. We . . . lost my father in an accident fifteen years ago. The same accident which robbed Pete '—she smiled in his direction, knowing he was feeling excluded from the conversation to some ex-tent and knowing also how hurt and upset he was likely to be as a result—' of both his parents. He has lived with us ever since then,' she concluded, ' but until he can find suitable employment in or around Vanmouth we shall have to leave him to follow when he can.'

'What kind of opening are you looking for, Mr Bradley?' Celia was determined to be both friendly and helpful, although Pete's expression showed his definite desire to be on his way. She nodded as he told her of his recently acquired qualifications, frowning slightly, then nodding again as though satisfied. 'If you are prepared to go into industrial accounting,' she observed, 'there ought to be an opening for you somewhere. I should advise your taking the *Vanmouth Advertiser*. Almost everybody advertises in there if they require the services of anyone in a professional capacity.'

'And you were looking for another position, Sister Benyon?' Quentin asked directly, his smile deepening as Joy nodded. 'I don't think you'll have much trouble here,' he said. 'We always seem to be short of nurses and Sisters in the winter time. Height of summer, everyone is thrilled to be here, but it's a very different story when the winter gales are raging, especially at St Lucy's. Being so close to the coastline and so high up they get the full benefit of every storm. The General is a little more sheltered, but somewhat off the beaten track when it comes to what little gaiety there is in Vanmouth in the winter months, but a great deal depends on how close you wish to be to home. I've no doubt you'll be welcomed with open arms at either hospital, and now that I've seen you in action'—he grinned suddenly, making his somewhat serious-looking face suddenly boyish—'I can add my own personal recommendation to whatever others you may have.'

'I think St Lucy's would be the best from my point of view,' Joy told them, suddenly feeling that with Doctor Moyser and his mother she could be perfectly frank. 'I have an invalid sister, you see,' she explained. 'At least, she isn't exactly an invalid, but she can't walk. She was involved in an accident three years or so ago, and since then she appears to have lost the use of her legs, although we have been to several specialists and they all say there's no physical reason why she should have done.'

'Then let's hope that by coming to Vanmouth you're able to find the impetus needed,' Quentin said cheerfully.

'My father is the consultant pathologist at St Lucy's. We might see what he can suggest. That's if you care to, of course.'

'I'd try anyone, anything,' Joy said rashly but meaning every word. 'Lana is such a lovely person, and until this happened she was also a lively, happy person as well. Now it seems '—she hesitated a moment then, sure of being understood, plunged on—' as though she has shut herself up inside with her injury . . . she doesn't seem to be able to make any effort. I know depression is something we have to fight separately from the injury itself, but it worries all of us, Mother, the twins, myself and '—she smiled at Pete again, trying to draw him into the circle of conversation—' Pete too.'

'I'm sure it does.' Celia spoke firmly. 'It must make life quite a strain all the time. Does that mean you would prefer not to live in at the Nurses' Home?'

They talked on throughout another cup of fresh tea and the time it took for them to smoke through a cigarette, then they heard the sound of another car outside and the slam of the outer door. There was a quick, brisk tread along the hall and into the lounge, and they were face to face with Lionel Moyser, Quentin's father and the husband of Celia.

Lionel Moyser was a well-set-up figure of a man, giving a living promise of what his son might reasonably become in the years which lay ahead. There were the same broad shoulders, the same height and the same thin face with the curiously slanting eyes, and there lay the greatest difference, apart from that of age, between father and son. Lionel's eyes were of a steel-blue, but his son's were a replica of Celia Moyser's bright, hazel brown ones.

Introductions were quickly made, and they were all relieved to hear that the young man on the bicycle was making 'satisfactory progress', a term which meant little to Pete but appeared to content the others. They chatted together for a few minutes longer, but Lionel had just finished a long, hard day and was tired, and Joy and Pete were only too conscious of the drive home which lay ahead of them.

'I'll telephone Mr Anderson again as soon as you're on the road,' Quentin promised. 'He said he wouldn't be going to bed for hours and that when you left, if I phoned again he would tell your mother so that she would know approximately what time to expect you.'

Joy thanked him, took her place beside Pete, very conscious of Quentin's eyes which seemed to promise so much of excitement and who knew what else in the future, then the little car was speeding down the drive and out on to the main road on the first stage of the journey back to Wilborough.

They drove in silence for some distance. Joy took two cigarettes from her case in her handbag, although she had already smoked the quota she allowed herself daily, lit them and passed one to Pete. Apart from a murmured 'thanks' there was still no word between them, until she felt she must break the silence, must talk to someone about these strangers who had entered so unexpectedly into their lives and who, she felt, would make an impact in some way which would be, so far as she was concerned, quite unforgettable.

'Friendly people, aren't they?' she said lightly. 'And I liked the Wrenshaws too. I've a feeling we're going to be amongst real friends when we eventually settle in Vanmouth.'

'They're a sight too friendly, considering we've only just met them, so far as I'm concerned,' Pete said in an antagonistic voice so unlike his usual cheery tones that Joy felt herself turn automatically in his direction, in some concern. 'I didn't like the way that young doctor was looking at you,' Pete growled. 'I suppose they're all alike, so used to all you nurses and Sisters and what-have-you looking up to them as though they're little tin gods or something. . . .'

He broke off as Joy's merry laughter rang out, startling him. She had been thinking of the two house surgeons with whom she had dealt for the greater part of her time at Wilborough General, the one married and with a wife so fond of a gay time that he was always worried about how to keep up with her, the other disappointed in

54

love and vowing for the future that the only women who would interest him would be exceptional surgical cases.

'You've got entirely the wrong idea, Pete,' she told him. 'I suppose Doctor Quentin—he did tell us to call him that so's we didn't get mixed up between him and his father, didn't he?—was only looking at me, if indeed he looked at all, because I'd acted with what he would consider "due promptitude" when the accident happened to that unfortunate boy on the bicycle.'

'That wasn't how it seemed to me.'

Pete was by no means mollified, and for a time they continued to drive along in silence once more. There was very little traffic. Occasionally the odd heavy long-distance lorry passed them, and when Joy made the comment that 'knights of the road or not, they certainly know how to make those monsters move' Pete's only answer was another non-committal grunt.

Joy did not mind. She was content to sit quietly beside him, watching the road ahead in the beam of Pete's headlights, thinking of her unexpected meeting with Quentin Moyser and not allowing herself to dream too much about what she thought—and secretly hoped —she had read in his intent gaze.

'Don't be an idiot, Joy Benyon,' she told herself severely. 'For all you know he might well have a girl-friend or a fiancée—or maybe even a wife—tucked away somewhere, an attractive man like that!'

A girl friend or even a fiancée might well be a surmountable obstacle, but if he were married . . .

'It doesn't seem likely,' she thought, but she shivered slightly as the idea sped through her mind, 'not when he's obviously living at home with his parents.'

'Cold, Joy?' Pete had noted the shiver as, she thought in some compunction, he appeared to notice any and everything which might be adversely affecting any one of the family.

'Not really, thanks.' She took the rug he dragged from the back of the car and tucked it about herself to satisfy his instinct for caring for someone in his care.

55

' Just . . . how do they say it? Someone walked over my grave.'

Pete gave her a curious glance but made no comment, and the remainder of their journey passed in almost companionable silence, except that Joy, for the first time in all the years Pete had been with them during which time she had driven thousands of miles by his side, felt a sense of strain and tension which had never before been present.

' Pure emotional imagination,' she told herself firmly as the lights of the outskirts of Wilborough came into view. ' I'm overtired after such a full day. That must be it.'

Just the same, when the suburb of Wilborough in which the General Infirmary was placed behind them and they were heading quickly for their own part of the town, she felt a sudden urge to be safely in her own small room, tucked up in bed, and free to think about Quentin Moyser, the house at Vanmouth and all the things which had happened to her since Mr Belding had appeared at the hospital.

' Come with me to take the car away, Joy,' Pete invited as he turned into Cranberry Terrace. ' It's always a help, negotiating that corner in the dark.'

In common with most of the houses in similar roads in Wilborough the garages at the back of the houses had been added as an afterthought when motoring became a popular mode of transport. Consequently there was not always much room to drive into the garages erected opening out on to the back lanes of the terraces, and Cranberry Terrace was no exception.

' All right,' Joy agreed cheerfully. ' Don't blow your horn—it's after hours. I'll just give one ring on the bell and then Mum'll know we're back. I always do that when I'm coming in late.'

She hurried out of the car and gave one sharp press to the bell in the door, then she was back in the car and beside Pete again even as the hall light came on and she knew Aileen was waiting, ready to put a match to the gas.

'Been quite a day.' The car was safely in the garage and Joy stood by the folding doors at the back, waiting for Pete to reach up and to lock them. 'But I've enjoyed it.'

He pulled the doors closed, reached up for the bolt, then, before she could move, his arms came down and were around her. For a moment Joy felt herself stiffen, then she tried to pull herself from his grasp, but she struggled in vain, and after a moment or so, feeling that such a struggle between herself and Pete was both a ridiculous and an undignified affair, she stood absolutely still.

'That's better.' Pete's voice was *almost* normal, but his hold on her slender form did not slacken, and she could feel his breath on her cheek, even though she turned her head.

'Joy,' he went on, suddenly breaking the strained silence which had fallen between them, 'this isn't the way I wanted—intended—things to be, not at all. But somehow events recently have pushed me into this. I don't just mean what happened tonight. I mean everything that's happened since Miss Barnes left her house and her money to you.'

'It doesn't make any difference to . . . any of us, Pete,' Joy said firmly, although she knew she was not speaking the truth. It was going to make a great deal of difference, not only to herself but to all of them, Pete included.

'It does.' Pete was normally a quiet, non-argumentative young man, but just now he was stirred as Joy had never known him to be stirred before. 'It means, for one thing, that you, all of you, will be going away, going out of my life, unless I'm lucky enough to find some way of following you all later on . . . and that doesn't seem very likely at the present moment. But you know I shall follow you all just as soon as ever I can. You're all the family I've got, Joy. Not that I'm worried about them—although I'm fond enough of you all, you know that. But it's *you* I'm thinking of. Just you, Joy.'

'You can come over and see us, just as soon as we

get settled, Pete.' She tried desperately to put things back on their old familiar footing, but he would not listen.

'That isn't what I mean at all,' he said doggedly, ' and you know quite well that it isn't. I hadn't intended to say anything like this to you for ages. Not for a few years yet, anyway. Mr Simpson promised me a partnership in the firm if I " showed promise ", and I was quite content to try and work hard and work up to that in time. Mr Abbicombe, the insurance broker, told me he could arrange for me to borrow enough money to put into the firm when the time came, and a reasonable way of repayment. Oh,' he said with a sudden and totally unexpected bitterness she found strangely touching, ' I'd got it all worked out. I was going to wait until I could have something to show you, something to prove I'd be able to take care of you, to take some of the burdens of the twins and their education, their future, some of the care of Lana from your shoulders . . . and then this Miss Barnes has to come along and leave you with a house of your own, something I can't hope to give you for years and years, and then only with a mortgage tacked on to it, if we're lucky enough to get a mortgage, that is —and enough money to keep the place going, without it costing you as much as things are costing you now !'

'Pete, I . . .'

'I know.' He gave a despairing groan which was instantly shattered by his next spate of words which seemed to come tumbling over themselves in an effort to make her understand. 'I'm glad for you, for all of you. You know that. That was a big enough pill to swallow on its own account, knowing you could go on being as independent as the old lady herself, to the end of your own days if you wished, without what happened tonight. When we met that Doctor Quentin and I saw the way he looked at you, I knew right away things were going to be . . . wrong for me, right from now onwards. He fell for you, Joy. I don't blame him. But you don't know anything about him ! He's good-looking. He seems to have money, and everything his heart could wish for, including a nice home, good parents and all the rest of it. Why isn't he married and established in a home of his own somewhere, with a wife to look after his welfare and his practice or whatever you call it? Maybe he's just a gay philanderer, and you're going the right way to let him break your heart!'

The ready colour flew into Joy's cheeks. Surely she had not looked at young Doctor Quentin in any way likely to give Pete cause for what was tantamount to an accusation of flirting?

'You have no right to say such things,' she told him angrily. 'We've only just met the doctor and his family, and they're very charming and friendly people. There's no necessity whatsoever for all this sort of thing! You may be almost like an elder brother so far as I'm concerned, but I intend to live my own life. . . .'

'That's just it,' Pete burst in, equally angrily. 'I'm *not* your brother, and I don't look upon you as a sister either! I've thought about this ever since your mother agreed to let me undertake articles. I could have done some other job, maybe some manual work on the buildings or in a factory, and made enough money to set up a house a lot sooner than this. But I was working on a long-term policy, on something that's going to be with me all my life, even if there are slumps again or anything like that. I might even try for Inland Revenue work. There'll always be people with my kind of training there, and opportunities for promotion.'

'I couldn't agree more.' Gently but firmly Joy managed to disengage herself from Pete's arms until she stood just a little apart from him. 'Don't think I'm being unkind, Pete,' she said gently. 'It's just that I've never thought of you—of anyone—in this way, and this has been an emotional and sufficiently exhausting day as it is without all this at its ending! It won't be long before we're both getting up to go to work,' she reminded him. 'Put all this behind you for the time being, there's a good lad. Mother and Lana and Cousin Emma will all be waiting to hear what the house is like and all about everything, so it's going to be ages before we get to bed.'

'Mother, Lana, Cousin Emma and the twins!' Pete said, still angry, but now there was a bitterness in his tone which had not been there earlier. 'You're always the same, Joy. That's what makes me love you, I think. You always think of all the others first, just as you've always lumped me in and along with them . . . what's best for all has always been your ideal. It's a wonderful thing, this family feeling, but it's *you* I'm thinking of! I love you, Joy. . . .'

He moved forward and would have taken her in his arms again, but she was too quick for him. Deftly she moved towards the small door which led into the tiny suburban garden.

'You don't,' she said gently. 'You're just . . . used to me, used to my being there all the time. You'll meet some other girl, maybe before we expect it, with only herself and her own affairs to think about.'

'That's what I'm trying to tell you.' Pete moved to stand beside her, his tone pleading. 'You never know, your mother might meet someone yet. She's a lovely, charming woman. The twins'll grow up. They'll leave you and lead their own lives! Lana doesn't care about you or anyone else nowadays, but she'd be off like a shot if she met a wealthy man who was interested in her . . . and Cousin Emma'll not mind anything, so long as someone looks after her and she can make herself a little useful in return.'

'I won't listen.' Joy put her hands over her ears and opened the door. 'In the morning you'll be sorry you said all this tonight,' she prophesied, 'and I'll be willing to forget it . . . but I meant what I said, Pete. Remember that. I've always looked on you as a brother, and that's how I'm sure I shall always think of you. I'll tell Mother you'll be along in a minute, shall I?' and without waiting for a reply she turned and hurried into the house as fast as she possibly could.

CHAPTER VII

The last month the little family were to spend at Cranberry Terrace seemed to be crammed in every moment, there was so much to do. Pete had taken himself off to Mrs Parrott's house on the other side of the road, the morning after he and Joy had paid their first visit to Fernbank. Aileen, who had grown to look upon him as a member of her own family, was a little hurt at first, but after Lana and Joy, to say nothing of Emma, had said all they had to say on the subject, she seemed a little more contented.

'It's only likely the boy'll want to get settled in while you're still here to turn to if things don't work out just as he has hoped and planned,' Emma said philosophically. 'He's a young man now, Aileen, not the boy you took in, shattered and forlorn by what had happened to him He knows he'll have to fend for himself now he's more or less on his feet, and he knows he has you and this family to thank for that—and it's only likely he'll want to make sure he'll be as comfortable as he expected across at Mrs Parrott's. If he isn't I dare say he'll be back here, asking you to help him find somewhere else before you leave for Vanmouth. He knows you have all sorts of connections in the business world, and he'll very likely be back before you know it to take advantage of the fact.'

'He knows Mrs Parrott has two nieces who have done very well for themselves. He's probably got an eye to the main chance,' Lana contributed a little scathingly. 'Didn't one of the girls win some sort of small fortune in a fashion competition or something not so very long ago?'

'I don't think that sort of thing interested Pete very much,' Joy had said before she gave any thought to the conversation. Lana gave her a curious glance.

'Don't you believe it, love.' She sounded bored and disillusioned. 'Money in the bank or the pocket, or the prospects of a partner whose earning capacity can equal his own, means a lot to every ambitious young man. I know the girl who's Tony's main model has worked with him on the contract I'd had my eye on in those two fashion magazines, and they're pulling in a nice fat salary each out of those alone . . . that was how *we'd* planned it,' she ended bitterly, ' and that goes for almost every man, in my opinion. If you'd been left the *value* of this house and its contents, instead of more or less having to live in the place and look after whoever it was you tell us cares for the house and grounds, as well as the rest of us, Pete wouldn't have thought twice about asking *you* to marry him! With capital behind him he could start up on his own account, and that's where the money's made in his line of country.'

Continuing to get ready to leave for the bus from the end of the terrace which took her to the bottom of the hill where the General was situated, Joy felt a sudden surge of thankfulness that she had not confided in Lana about Pete's astonishing outburst on their return from Vanmouth. She was about to go through the door when Lana spoke again.

' By the way,' she asked casually, ' what about this doctor friend of yours, the one you met when you went to see Fernbank? Has he got any money, do you know?'

Joy felt the warm colour in her cheeks and hastily stooped as though to attend to the laces of her sensible ward shoes, but when she spoke she was relieved to note nothing of the turbulence of emotions which shook her at the mention of Doctor Quentin sounded in her voice.

' I'm afraid I don't know anything about his personal affairs,' she said stiffly. ' I've no doubt you'll be able to discover all you want to know when once we get there. He'll be your doctor, you know. I thought you would rather we all went to him as our family doctor than the only other one in that area.'

' I don't really mind.' Disinterest was back in Lana's voice. ' I don't suppose either of them will be able to do anything for me, any more than Doctor Frankton and the hospitals round here have been able to do. I just thought it might be worth while . . . cultivating his friendship.'

Joy went out at that point, giving the door an unnecessarily sharp slam behind her. How different Lana was since her accident! She knew a long illness, or a long time of being in bed and with little or nothing to do, often played queer tricks on the personalities of people, but she had never expected her own sister to change in quite such a fashion.

'She doesn't mean it,' Joy told herself firmly as she boarded her bus, but the nagging thought persisted that Lana did indeed mean what she said, and though her scope might be limited, tied as she was to her bed or day couch, there was no denying the fact that she looked even more beautiful than ever, since her long inactivity and stay indoors had given her a delicate, fragile air which was undoubtedly appealing.

With an effort Joy dismissed all worrying thoughts of home from her mind as she began her work of the day. Tomorrow she and Pete were summoned to the court in Vanmouth where the case of the boy on the bicycle and the lorry and trailer which had hit him was to be heard. Matron had been most helpful about arranging time off for Joy to attend the court, but she was certainly not looking forward to the trip with Pete, not after what had happened when they returned home last time!

She need not have worried. Pete was just as friendly and as helpful as he had always been when he tooted the horn of the little car outside their door the following day. He made no references to Doctor Quentin or to his own affairs, but kept the conversation going on topics of everyday interest obviously culled from the morning's paper.

They arrived at the court in good time and were shown where to sit. Doctor Quentin was there and he waved to them, but Pete neither moved nor spoke. The case was soon over, and Joy realized that her unspoken fears of acting as a witness to an accident had been completely without foundation. The lorry-driver was exonerated

63

from blame, and as the boy, a certain Tom Robinson, was still in hospital he was not there to hear the warning given by the magistrate to boys who tried to hang on to the backs of moving vehicles to help them along the road.

Doctor Quentin was waiting for them outside the court. He greeted them with a friendly smile and looked appreciatively at Joy in her smart navy and white mufti.

'If you care to run up to The Poplars,' he told them, 'that's the name of our house, Mother said would you care to join us for lunch? If you would rather call at Fernbank, I know Mrs Wrenshaw will be able to dish up something choice in a matter of minutes, she loves to do things like that, but you'll be very welcome at home, I do assure you.'

'Thank you very much,' Pete answered before Joy had time to choose which would give least offence to the two women she had already decided she liked very much, Mrs Moyser and Mrs Wrenshaw, 'but I thought we might be a little pushed for time and so I took the liberty of ordering a lunch for us both over the telephone this morning. I've booked a table at that restaurant I saw on the corner when we came before, the Golden Pheasant.'

'And a very good meal they serve too,' Quentin said without rancour. 'When do you hope to move in?' He spoke directly to Joy so that this time Pete had to remain silent.

'The first of June,' she told him, 'or, to be more precise, the last day of May. That will give me a week at home to help Mother with the packing and whatnot. It also means that if we're out of Cranberry Terrace *before* June the first, Mother gets one third of the quarterly rent returned, since they have someone waiting to come in. That should just about pay for the removal and the ambulance.'

'Ambulance?' Quentin's brows shot up, then he nodded, smiling. 'Oh, yes, for your sister. Will you leave that for me to arrange, Miss Benyon? I think I may be able to help.' He half turned away and then

64

back to her again. ' By the way,' he said, ' I haven't heard of your being over for interview at St Lucy's. You aren't waiting until you are settled, are you?'

' I've an appointment there for this afternoon,' Joy informed him. ' The Matron at Wilborough telephoned through for me this morning. She thought it better than having to make another journey or leave it until we arrived here.'

' I agree.' Quentin nodded again and once more turned back to his own car. ' Good luck,' he said cheerfully. ' You'll get on very well with Enid Penrose. She's a charming woman. Leave the ambulance to me, don't forget, and we'll look forward to seeing you before long.'

He was gone with a cheery wave of the hand, and Joy was not conscious of staring after his car until Pete gave her an ungentle and brotherly prod to attract her attention.

' If you want to be on time for your appointment,' he said crisply, ' then we'd better get a move on in finding our bearings for that restaurant again!'

It was not long before they were seated at a small table for two in the lovely restaurant of Pete's choice. When she looked around her and cast a quick, experienced eye at the prices on the menu, Joy immediately offered to ' go Dutch ', but with a lordly gesture Pete waved the offer on one side, and, wisely, she refrained from saying anything more.

The meal was perfect and excellently served. How she repressed a shiver when the bill was presented to Pete Joy never knew, but Pete accepted it calmly, counted out some money from his wallet and, as yet another gesture, she was certain, laid a generous tip on the plate.

' I'll drive you to the gates of the hospital,' he offered, ' then I'm going to take a walk around the town for an hour or so before I come back for you. I just wanted to see what sort of openings there are likely to be in my line, if I ever decide to follow you all.'

' Very well.' Joy forbore to say he needn't bother

about looking for accommodation as well. She wasn't sure as yet that she wanted Pete back as a member of their household. It would be different if he ever found some other girl. She'd rejoice with him then as, one day, she hoped she'd rejoice when Rex found a girl of his own with whom he'd be happy to spend the rest of his life and who would be right for him. But not just yet!

Pete drove off and left her, and Joy found herself being shown into a small waiting room by a pretty young cadet nurse, and told that Matron would see her in a moment.

Matron did not ring for her quite so quickly as that, but she certainly did not keep the girl waiting, and as she was shown into the small office with the single word 'Matron' on the door, Joy wondered just what sort of woman she would be working under this time.

The first minutes of her meeting with Enid Penrose were enough to convince her that Quentin Moyser had been quite right when he had said she would 'get on very well' with her new boss. Enid Penrose had taken the Matronship of St Lucy's at a remarkably young age, but she dealt ably and firmly with her responsibilities, and did not allow them to narrow her own life or the lives of those about her.

Joy understood her at once. She was a woman with all the knowledge and dignity demanded of her profession, a woman who, if immediate impressions were to be trusted, was in exactly the right job. She loved her work and her brain was quick, clear and alert. She was young, but she knew the value of discipline, both for herself and for her staff, yet there was nothing of the dictator about her in any shape or form.

She glanced quickly but carefully at Joy's letters and testimonials, her certificates of qualification, then looked up, smiling from a long-lashed pair of very dark brown eyes.

'We're at present without a regular Sister on the Maternity Block, Sister Benyon,' she told Joy. 'I suggest you begin there, if that is agreeable to you?

66

You will, of course, change round as time passes. You can study our working rota at your leisure. I have a copy here.' She handed Joy a neatly typed page. 'I understand that you wish to live at home.'

'Please, Matron,' Joy said. 'I promise that what I do at home won't interfere with my work at St Lucy's. I didn't allow it to at Wilborough General, and I had quite a way to travel on the bus every morning.'

'You will at least be close at hand here,' Matron agreed, 'if, as I understand it, Fernbank is to be your new home. One or two other people from here also live along that road and come in daily. You may be able to arrange some form of regular transport with one or other of them.'

'I hope, in time, to buy a little car of my own.' Joy surprised herself by the statement, but all at once it seemed the obvious thing to do. With the rent and rates now taken care of, there would surely be enough for her to run a small vehicle for herself, since previously it had been the running costs of the thing which had been a deterrent to such a purchase.

'An excellent idea,' Enid Penrose nodded. 'There's a very good school of motoring in the town, if you don't drive already.'

'Not yet,' Joy said. 'Thank you.'

They chatted a little longer, then Matron rose, touching the bell on her desk.

'I expect you would like to see round the hospital first,' she enquired, shaking hands. 'I'll have Cadet Ronsome take you round, and I shall look forward to having you report here on the first of June.'

'I'm going to like her, very much,' Joy surprised herself by the realization. 'Just how did Quentin Moyser know she was just my sort of person?'

There wasn't time for any further speculation along those lines. She followed her guide through St Lucy's, little Cadet Ronsome a little overawed by being delegated to conduct the new Sister around the premises. She liked what she saw. The hospital was not old but not really new. There were two new wings, one of which contained the maternity block of which Matron had spoken. There were many up-to-date clinics of all descriptions for outpatients, and the staff she encountered seemed pleasant and charming people.

She thanked her guide and went outside to wait for Pete on one of the wooden forms which dotted the entrance to the hospital, but she had not been there many minutes before he came speeding back to brake in a little cloud of dust beside her.

'Everything all right,' he asked, beaming as she nodded. 'Good. I've had a sort of adventure too.' He switched on the engine and the car began gently to descend the gradual hill. 'I was looking round, as I said I would, and all at once a little dog dangling a long length of ribbon behind it came pelting down the road, obviously pleased to be out on its own! I'd caught hold of the ribbon before I realized there was a girl trying to catch the dog. She was breathless and upset, but very glad to get the little beggar back. Said it was a birthday present to her mother or something and that she'd begged to be allowed to take it out. Seems she's used to big dogs, never thought a little ball of fluff like that could have ideas of its own. Anyhow '—he put out the indicator and headed the little car in the direction of Wilborough—'the incident might have done me some good. She says her father's a local business man, and she'd have a word with him as to what prospects there might be for me around here, so I gave her Mrs Parrott's address and I'm hoping. . . . How did you get on?'

Discussion about the hospital, Matron Penrose and the girl with the dog whose name Pete was annoyed with himself to discover he'd forgotten to ask lasted them most of the way home. By that time Joy had decided the episode of the night they had first been to see Fernbank was over and forgotten between them, but when she invited Pete in to share their evening meal as he had done all these long years past, he shook his head.

'I'd rather not, Joy, thank you all the same,' he said

quietly. ' I don't want to upset you any more before you go. I've enjoyed today,' he added unexpectedly, ' and I hope it won't be long before I'm back with you all again, then things can go on as they used to do.'

' Maybe so,' Joy agreed as they said goodnight and she turned into her home alone, but she knew in her heart that things would never ' go on ' between herself and Pete in the old way, not ever again, and somehow she hoped with all her heart that he might encounter someone else, someone like the girl whose dog had run away, in whom he could really be interested and who would be interested in him and with whom he could and would fall deeply and sincerely in love.

There was little further time to worry about either Pete or anyone else. Her goodbyes to Marcia and the others at the Wilborough General had to be said, her farewell made to Matron, then she was walking down the steep hill and to the bus home for the very last time.

The week which followed was a chaotic blur ever afterwards in Joy's mind. She had not realized that in almost twenty years of living in one house, a family could collect so much stuff which was not worth their while to take with them when they left! At last everything was sorted, crated and packed. The great day arrived, and Mr Anderson came down to their house to tell them Doctor Quentin had telephoned to say the ambulance would be along in about half an hour.

' I don't want to get there first and be all by myself with a pair of strangers!' Lana wailed, and refused to be consoled until Joy volunteered to ride in the ambulance with her and would, therefore, be there when Lana arrived.

The moving van, a very large one, went off with the twins sitting at the front with the driver and his mate. Aileen, who had said she and Cousin Emma would travel down by train, was surprised and obviously more than a little touched when, at the last moment, just as she was saying an almost tearful farewell to Mrs Jarvis who had been her neighbour for twenty years, Pete arrived and announced that he had managed to get the afternoon off and would drive Aileen and Emma in the wake of the ambulance and the furniture van.

The ambulance went first, and the last Joy saw of Cranberry Terrace was the furniture van outside the door of her late home, her mother and Cousin Emma standing by Pete's mini, and those neighbours with whom they had grown friendly over the years offering advice and help whether it was wanted or not.

The journey, so far as the ambulance and the driver and his helper were concerned, was quite uneventful, but Lana, who could see nothing from where she lay, grew bored and fretful as the miles sped by. It was all in vain for Joy to talk to her of the beauties of the May countryside through which they were speeding. She could see nothing of it, and although Joy opened the windows so that the scent of the freshly growing countryside could reach her, Lana still grumbled and remained irritable throughout the long journey.

Joy was heartily thankful when the ambulance at last turned in at the Shore Road. In a few minutes, she thought, she would be able to distract Lana's attention from the slight discomforts of the journey, and in new surroundings and amongst new faces, it would not be long before her sister set out to charm everyone, as she always did. The ambulance stopped at the gates of Fernbank, and to Joy's unutterable relief she saw Quentin Moyser leave his own car across the road and station himself at the gates of the house as the men opened the doors of the ambulance and prepared to lift Lana out.

Accustomed as she was to the effect of her sister's undeniable beauty on those who encountered it for the first time, in some way it had never occurred to Joy to think of what possible effect Lana might have on Quentin. She need not, she felt, wait for words. One look at his face as he smiled down at the fragile figure on the stretcher seemed enough to tell her all she wanted to know. With a muttered word or two about going inside to tell Mrs Wrenshaw they had arrived, she left them, Quentin still standing at the head of the stretcher, but as she talked to the sympathetic housekeeper and her husband, she felt the first cloud pass over what had seemed such a cloudless and promising future not only for her little family, but for her own happiness in the days which lay ahead.

CHAPTER VIII

There was little time for introspection that first evening. The twins and Aileen, and Cousin Emma too despite the fact that her rheumatism was paining her rather more than usual, insisted on a complete tour of the house, from the deep, mysterious old-fashioned cellars to the attics themselves.

'You go ahead and take your dear ma round, Miss Joy,' Mrs Wrenshaw insisted. 'I'll get some tea ready for everyone. I have most of it ready, so it won't take many minutes, but you'll have time for a quick sort of general inspection, as it were. I hope,' she went on anxiously, 'you don't mind me calling you Miss Joy and Miss Lana? You see, when the three Miss Barnes were all here it seemed easier to say Miss Muriel, Miss Una and Miss Laura rather than to have to say a great deal more to make certain their father knew which one I was talking about.'

'We don't mind in the least,' Joy assured her. Lana, she noted, was already talking animatedly to Quentin, who had drawn up a chair by the side of her couch. 'Come along, Mum,' she invited, leading the way up the wide stairs. She must not, she reminded herself firmly, look as though the attention Lana was already receiving was hurting her as quickly as this! In an effort to show she was totally carefree, she hurried her little party from room to room, scarcely conscious that Pete had installed himself at the tail end of the procession and was making his usual careful survey of his surroundings.

'If nobody else wants it,' Aileen said wistfully as they came back to the ground floor, 'I'd like very much to have the room you said was the morning-room in the old days, as a bed-sitting-room or else a small office. I looked round as we came through, and there appears to be plenty of scope for a secretarial bureau.'

'There's a great deal more in the town itself, Mrs Benyon,' Pete confirmed. 'I think it'll go like a bomb!'

'If I can build up a nice steady business that will do for me,' Aileen said firmly. 'I'm not like you young things, wanting the earth on a platter in under five minutes!'

Laughing and talking together, with Mr and Mrs Wrenshaw reluctantly consenting to take their tea with the friendly family, Joy soon forgot the slight unease which had swept over her when she had first seen Quentin and her sister together.

Quentin, who had accepted a cup of tea but refused to eat, saying that his mother would have prepared a meal and would be expecting him at home, came abruptly from Lana's side and stood beside Joy's chair, stooping so that he could speak under the cover of the conversation without any of the others hearing what he had to say.

'What a beautiful girl your sister is,' he began. 'It's more than a shame she should be tied to that couch or her bed! I honestly don't think she need be housebound much longer, though. I've had a chat with her, and she's to come to St Lucy's in the morning for an examination. We'll know then if my diagnosis is confirmed or not. If it is, then I'm certain we will be able to help her. She's hurt inside,' he added abruptly. 'We must find her some means of wanting to live again, to belong.'

'That's what the other doctors have said, I told you,' Joy answered quietly. 'It's my own firm conviction as well. But I've tried everything I can think of.'

'Then we must think of something else, mustn't we?' Quentin commented agreeably, placing his cup on the table and preparing to leave. 'I'll see you tomorrow evening, maybe,' he said before he left. 'I do casualty duty one morning and two evenings a week at St Lucy's. They're very short-staffed, you know.'

Joy made no comment, and the twins, who had taken to Doctor Quentin without any reservations, accompanied him to the door. Joy looked across at where Lana was lying, an open book on her knees, but her sister was not looking at the opened page. She was staring into space and a strange little smile played round the corners of her lovely mouth, just as though, Joy thought bemusedly, she had secret dreams of her own which she could not or would not share with any of them.

Pete left early, as he had only been granted the afternoon free from business and still had the drive back. Aileen looked questioningly at Joy as he rose to go, but Joy made no move, and it was left to Aileen to see him off. She came back to the others, a little sad, for after all these years it was like seeing one of her own family leave the nest and she felt much as she had done when Joy had gone off to do her training.

'Pete seems delighted with the place and the town,' she reported. 'I don't think it will be long before he's found a niche for himself around these parts. Thank goodness there's plenty of room in Fernbank. There's even a little shed at the bottom of the garden where he can do all the pottering he wants to do with his car, his bits of woodwork and his photography and the like without getting in anyone else's way.'

'I'm going up to bed, if you don't mind, Mother.' Joy bent and kissed Aileen goodnight. 'I think everyone knows where he or she is to sleep and all the rest of it. I want an early start to my day tomorrow. I don't intend to be late!'

'And we'll have an early start doing something about all this excess of furniture and what-have-you,' Aileen spoke to Mrs Wrenshaw as she too rose to follow her daughter. 'Whatever else we do, though'—she glanced round the dining-room at the dark red paper, the brown glossy paint—'we must do something to lighten and brighten this place up a little. I can't *bear* to live in drab surroundings.'

'There's a man—a retired man—lives just down Russet Drive,' Mrs Wrenshaw informed them. 'He's very good at paper-hanging and painting and all that sort of thing. Been in the decorating business all his life, and he only said last week he was bored to tears since he had retired . . . he might welcome a job like this where he could take his time. You wouldn't want

74

it all done in a great hurry, would you?' she ended anxiously.

'My goodness, no!' Aileen laughed. 'That would be both too great an upheaval and too expensive. One room at a time, starting'—she wrinkled her brow—'in here, I think. But we can go into all that tomorrow. Lana dear, Mrs Wrenshaw has made up your bed in what apparently used to be the study. You can have your couch wheeled from there into the conservatory and from there out into the garden on fine, warm days. Cousin Emma will sleep downstairs too, there's a charming alcove in what's now to be your bedroom, and it just takes a three-quarter bed. You won't be alone at night then, and also it will save Cousin Emma having to climb the stairs so often.'

The twins, who had been given adjoining bedrooms, went off first, protesting loudly that tomorrow they intended to move themselves and their possessions up to two of the attics. At last all was quiet and peaceful, and the household settled down to sleep, but Joy lay wide awake for a long time, listening to the sound of the sea which was sufficiently close as to be soothing and yet far enough away not to be, at this time of the year at any rate, disturbing.

If coming to Vanmouth meant new life for Lana, then it was indeed wonderful, and she would be grateful to Miss Barnes to the end of her days. If their coming to Vanmouth was going to bring happiness to Quentin Moyser, if he was going to find his happiness with the lovely Lana whom he was so certain he could help to recovery, then Joy was happy for his sake. It would be enough, she told herself, and at the time she firmly believed it, knowing little of the ways and wounds of love, if she could know *he* was happy and that Lana loved him as Joy felt certain he would love Lana. The adoration, she told herself, was there in his eyes as he looked at her, as it had been in the eyes of so many men, ever since Lana entered her teens.

But Lana had a hard streak which only those who knew and loved her well realized was there. Lana loved money and the power money brought. She joked about it, laughed about it, but all her life she had resented the fact that they were not rich people. Would she love Quentin enough not to mind that he was not unduly wealthy, that although, as he had told Joy, the practice was a good one, there was always a lot of money going out, and he was by no means a millionaire?

'I won't let her hurt him,' Joy vowed as she tried again to settle off to sleep, but even as she closed her eyes she knew there was as yet no answer to the question . . . what could she do to prevent such a disaster happening to the man to whom she herself was so suddenly and so deeply attracted?

She was up early and almost ready to leave the house when a young man driving a battered little two-seater ran down the path and knocked at the door. Joy, who had been on the point of opening the door to go out, stared up at him.

'Nigel Webster, at your service,' he noted the clean, crisp uniform and grinned at her. 'I'm a houseman at St Lucy's, Sister Benyon. Doctor Moyser senior asked me to call and collect you. There isn't enough accommodation up there at the hospital, so one or two of us live out. I can call for you whenever I'm not on night duty,' he added quickly, running ahead and opening the door of the car for her. 'Saves all that walk up the hill. It's pleasant enough, but a drag.'

'Nothing like the sharp, steep hill to Wilborough General though,' Joy said thankfully. 'I used to be quite breathless when I got to the top if I'd missed the early bus and was a little late. I intend to get some sort of vehicle for myself, though, now we're here. But,' she added disconsolately, 'I'll have to learn to drive first.'

'I'll teach you, if you like,' Nigel offered. 'We must get together and arrange it,' but although she thanked him Joy knew she would do no such thing. She would go to the motoring school of which she had been told. She didn't intend to start off her career at St Lucy's by having her name coupled with that of a young houseman, however friendly he appeared to be.

The day passed pleasantly and quickly enough. Joy saw nothing of her sister, although she heard from Nurse Byecroft, a friendly girl who appeared to know whatever was going on in all departments of St Lucy's, that Lana's appointment with the specialist was fixed for ten-thirty that morning.

When Joy returned home at the end of the day, being driven back to the shore road end by another friendly nurse who shared a car with her sister, it was to learn that Quentin had just called and left again.

'He said to tell you his diagnosis was correct,' Lana reported suspiciously. 'Just what did he mean by that? Does that mean I have to go into hospital again? He left a note for you . . . over there.' She pointed with one long, slender finger with its freshly painted nail.

'Thanks.' She ripped open the envelope and drew forth the single sheet of notepaper covered in a surprisingly clear and readable handwriting. It did not take many minutes to read the brief note, then she glanced across to where Lana was watching, openly suspicious of Quentin's verdict.

'Well?' Lana demanded as Joy still stared at the unmistakable signature 'Always yours, Quentin'. With an effort she pulled herself together and told herself not to be idiotic enough as to read meanings into things which were probably never intended. Maybe, since he was such a naturally friendly person, this was his customary method of signing letters which were personal rather than purely of business purpose.

'Doctor Quentin simply says he agrees with the specialist opinion and that a physiotherapist, a Miss Amy Calvin, will call here two mornings each week, beginning in the morning. Also a masseur, a Mr Hugh Tate, will call twice each week from now onwards, beginning the day after tomorrow, and that in a few weeks' time you should be able to attend the outpatients' department at St Lucy's, so,' she added more to herself than to Lana who had apparently lost interest once she knew

77

the verdict upon herself, ' I shall have to get my little car as quickly as possible and try and get enough lessons in to pass the test before you start there!'

' If Doctor Quentin and his father have as much influence as all that,' Lana retorted crisply, ' then I don't see why an ambulance can't come for me when I start with the clinic, if I ever do.'

' I think you will.' Joy suddenly was certain that this indeed was the beginning of a new phase for them all, Lana included. Just how or in what way Quentin's treatment was going to help she did not allow herself to stop and think, but somehow she was very certain things were going to change.

Her opinion did not alter as the days went by. Doctor Franklyn had always called once or twice each month, to check on Lana's general health and to try yet again to urge her to make the attempt to enter once more into general living. Nurse Brown, the friendly district nurse who had served the Wilborough area which embraced Cranberry Terrace, had called regularly to give Lana her bath and to see that lying in bed and on her couch so many hours of every day she did not develop sore patches on her skin, the curse of those confined to their beds for any length of time.

Now, she found, Doctor Quentin called in *every* day, seldom at the same time for two days in succession, but always, before the little household went to bed at night, his car had been parked outside, sometimes for only a few minutes, sometimes, often in the evenings, for an hour or more.

By the middle of June, when Lana's couch had been wheeled daily into the garden now bursting into a glorious mass of perfume and glowing colour, and Lana herself had begun to develop the beginnings of an attractive light tan, Joy found she was growing almost reconciled to the fact that Doctor Quentin was paying court to her sister, although Lana, having asked many questions and memorized the answers, about the difficulties of being the wife of a busy general practitioner, and about the income and outgo of a shared practice such

78

as Quentin had with his father, certainly offered him little encouragement.

'She's friendly and polite enough,' Joy mused one afternoon when she was off duty, 'but nothing more. And I'm not certain I can see any great improvement in her interest in living, though I must say her general health appears to have improved. Quentin must feel he's rather hitting his head against a brick wall, trying to rouse her from this deadly feeling of being reconciled to remaining a beautiful log to the end of her days.'

She said as much to Amy Calvin, whose visit that day had been put off to the afternoon. Joy had brewed a fresh pot of tea and called to the physiotherapist when she was about to leave. She liked Amy. She was a brisk, sensible person who regarded nothing and no one as being without hope. Her patience appeared to be without limits, and in every way she oozed encouragement in spite of Lana's lassitude and, so far, faint co-operation.

'If your sister were a patient in your ward, Sister Benyon,' she said as she accepted her tea and listened to Joy's words, 'you would feel great strides have been made. When the patient happens to be a member of one's own family, things always look a little different. I know, because I looked after my brother when he had an accident with his motor-bike. Once we get Lana to St Lucy's regularly I shall give her a little electrical treatment, with Doctor Quentin's approval, of course.'

'He's taking a very great interest in Lana as a patient, isn't he?' Joy asked artlessly. 'We're all very grateful, but I hope that doesn't mean he has to scamp his visits elsewhere.'

'He's certainly taking a more than customary interest in her case,' Amy confirmed, 'but I think that's only natural in the circumstances, don't you? He doesn't always stay as long as this,' she glanced out into the garden where Quentin was sitting on the hammock beside Lana's couch. 'Sometimes I've been here when he's looked in and gone almost straight away. But he

79

usually stays on the days you're here, Sister,' she added meaningly.

'Only to discuss Lana and her progress and one or two other patients of his I happen to have in my ward,' Joy smiled, and rose. She did not want to carry the discussion further. She could not have either Amy Calvin or anyone else reading a wrong meaning into the attention Quentin was paying to her sister!

'Whatever the reason he's a happier young man than he was before your family came to live at Fernbank,' Amy Calvin returned, 'and that's no understatement. Before that he was pleasant enough, friendly and happy enough, but now he seems to go about as though he's . . . well, it sounds silly, but as though he's inspired, driven by a purpose. Maybe it's the curing of your sister so that you'll have less worry.'

'Maybe,' Joy agreed, and began to stack the cups and dishes on to a tray to take into the kitchen. She did not want to speculate any further about what reasons Quentin might or might not have for doing his very best to make Lana like the rest of them, able to take part in things, share in the joys of living.

Amy had been gone only a few moments when Quentin walked in from the garden. Emma had carried out tea to Lana and the doctor, and he came in now, carrying the two empty cups. He looked critically at Joy as he set the cups carefully on the table.

'You're not doing too much, are you, Joy?' he queried. 'You don't look as though you're having the right amount of sleep!' He picked up her hand from her side and felt her pulse, and was, apparently, satisfied. 'You're sure all this isn't too much for you?' he pressed, gesturing round. 'Helping your mother organize her bureau, seeing to whatever Lana needs when you are home, keeping an eye on the twins and everything else in addition to your own work? I know things have been pretty hectic in the Maternity Block at Lucy's these last weeks.'

'I'm all right, really.' Joy took her hand away, afraid her leaping pulse might yet betray her secret. 'I was told this morning I'll be on Women's Medical in a week or so, starting as Night Sister. I've always liked nights . . . there's something soothing and quiet, un-rushed about the wards, unless, of course, there's an emergency. I shall soon be my bright and cheerful self,' she smiled. 'As soon as the twins have finished their exams! I find myself feeling for them, every time they go off to another one!'

'That's the crux of the matter,' Quentin smiled. 'You "feel" for everyone, your heart's too big, emo-tionally speaking! I shall have to keep an eye on you, have a word with the family and make certain you have the requisite amount of sleep and so on.'

'I shall,' she made herself smile again. 'They're very good about things like that. I tell you, Doctor, I'm looking forward to that spell on night duty, truly.'

'Glad to hear it.' He picked up his bag and prepared to leave, pausing at the door to smile and add: 'And what's wrong with "Quentin" when I come to see you? After all, I think of myself as the friend of you all!' and before she could think of an adequate reply he had lifted his hand in mock salute and gone, closing the door gently behind him.

CHAPTER IX

Contrary to her usual practice on night duty, Joy began to worry and fret. It had nothing whatsoever to do with the hospital itself, nothing to do with her duties there, and no connection at all with the night staff with whom she was quickly on friendly terms. The whole thing, she knew, was within her own mind.

During the long, quiet hours, when most of her patients were sleeping and when one of the others woke and was quickly and competently dealt with by the nurse on duty, she found herself thinking of Quentin Moyser. The thoughts, she realized, were mostly absurd, the sort of thoughts she had never had about any other man throughout her life.

She found herself wondering what he had been like as a baby, a little boy. She knew he had an elder brother, now a doctor with the Air Force and stationed abroad somewhere. She knew he had a sister about his own age, nursing with the Queen Alexandra's nurses somewhere abroad, but no more than that.

Had he always wanted to be a doctor? Had he, as she herself had felt the call to nursing, wanted to help those who suffered, right from the first days of understanding what suffering was and how much could be done to help?

Had he ever had a girl-friend? It was ridiculous to suppose otherwise. There might have been someone in his student days, and if there had been, what had become of her? What sort of a girl was she, what sort of girl appealed to him . . . now?

' You needn't worry about *that*,' she told herself firmly one night when the speculative thoughts refused to be quietened. ' Lana appeals to him, even anyone who didn't know the first thing about either of them can see that. And it's only to be expected. She's the loveliest thing I've ever seen . . . and she knows how to make the most of herself, even though she's still stuck on that couch.'

There was no denying that Lana, beautiful as she had always been, was even more beautiful now she had developed a tan, followed, somewhat reluctantly, the few exercises that Miss Calvin had been able to persuade her would not be too much exertion for her as yet. There was a new awareness about her now, a new alertness, which added to her charm. Only this week Amy Calvin had suggested that she learned to touch-type, and said she would arrange for a special typewriter to be loaned to her so that she could practise. The typewriter was especially built to help bedridden patients, and there could now be no excuse about the difficulty or weight of the machine after Amy had explained how many of her patients were leading useful and interesting lives after developing some such skill.

'You'll be able to help your mother then,' she had told Lana cheerfully. 'She was saying only the other day how much work was coming into the bureau now and that she would soon have to advertise for someone to help her. I'm sure there's something you could do. And Doctor Quentin thinks it would be a very wonderful help in your own recovery.'

Lana had not said anything, and neither had Joy, at the time, but now, in the quiet hours of the night, she thought about it and wondered just how many more suggestions Doctor Quentin had made or approved of of which she knew nothing.

'I shall have to do something about myself if this goes on much longer,' Joy told herself firmly. 'I'm not sleeping in the day, not half so much as I should, wondering if I'll miss his visit. And yet,' she realized abruptly, 'since I've been on night duty he has usually called in the evening, before I've gone out. It's only on the nights he does casualty duty here that he's called in the day . . .' but common sense told her to read nothing of any personal note into these matters.

She went off duty the next morning feeling, which was most unusual for her, worn out and ready to sleep the clock round. She had her meal with the other night nursing staff before she left the hospital and decided that this morning she would dispense with that extra cup of tea and biscuits Emma or Mrs Wrenshaw had ready for her by the time she arrived back at Fernbank.

She had another driving lesson booked for late afternoon, so she would have to get what sleep in she could long before then, otherwise she would not be as alert and as safety-conscious as she was normally, and, she told herself firmly, it was very important that she passed her driving test just as soon as she could. She was all right getting to and from Lucy's without a car, for one or another of the staff was always coming and going at more or less the same time, but it would be quite a different matter when Lana had to be taken to the out-patients' clinic, maybe every day, just at first!

Quentin—there he was, back in her mind again and quite without her having any intention of thinking about him—had agreed with Lana that there was no reason why she should not be taken and fetched by ambulance, as were so many other patients. But they, Joy thought stubbornly, were probably making every effort to get themselves fit and well, whereas Lana, despite Miss Calvin and Mr Tate's assurances that she could and would soon be completely cured, remained a victim of these dreadful bouts of depression which robbed her at once of any benefits already gained.

By the time she reached Fernbank her head was aching and her feet felt as though they did not belong to her. She changed her mind about the cup of tea, it looked so welcoming and fresh, and took some aspirin, then went up to her room, undressed quickly and got into bed, opening the window and drawing the curtains fully across to darken the bright light of the July day.

'My new machine came this morning, love,' Aileen informed her as she went through on her way to the little 'office' which was just under Joy's bedroom. 'You wouldn't believe how quiet it is, or how easy on the wrists! I shall not disturb you now, with all my clatter and whatnot underneath your floor.'

84

'I don't think you or anyone else will disturb me today, dear,' Joy said wearily. 'I think once these aspirins have begun to work I'll take some rousing to go back on duty tonight . . . or rather to get up for my driving lesson.'

Aileen looked at the girl's face, a little drawn in the bright light of morning, and at the unaccustomed dark patches below her eyes.

'I think you should let me ring and cancel that lesson, love,' she suggested. 'It isn't so important that you need to wreck your health. Give it a break until your next free day. When is it?'

'Wednesday,' said Joy, suddenly giving in. 'All right. I honestly don't feel up to it today. I'll be all right once I've had a decent rest.'

'I hope so.' Aileen smiled and Joy turned over to settle to sleep, but although the aspirin helped the headache it did nothing to prevent her thoughts whirling as they seemed to have done nothing *but* whirl ever since she had started her night duty.

She tossed and turned, for once envying Lana whose couch had been taken into the garden as Joy came home. There, amid the sweetly scented roses, the mignonette which was a relic of Mr Barnes' old-fashioned garden, the lavender and the pinks, Lana would breathe in the flower perfume, the scent of the sea, the golden sunlight. Joy did not envy her sister's life, but just at that moment she felt she would have given a great deal to be lying out there in the sweetly scented air, with nothing whatsoever to do but to relax.

'I could sleep then,' she thought tiredly.

Downstairs the door bell pealed. It was not the casual single ring of one of their now many friends in and around the town, almost all of whom knew Sister Benyon was 'on night duty' and would be sleeping, and who signalled their arrival by either a discreet tap on the door or a single brief peal of the bell. No, this was a prolonged ringing, as though whoever it was had kept his or her finger on the bell push and seemed likely to let it remain there until someone opened the door.

There were footsteps, footsteps muffled by the carpet in the hall. The door was opened and a man's loud voice drifted up the stairs and reached Joy as she strove in vain for the sleep which eluded her. She turned over again, searching in vain for a cool place on her sheet and pillow, and from directly underneath came the sound of the same loud, angry-toned voice.

Joy sat up in bed and did something she had never done before. She reached out for her handbag, took out a cigarette and lighted it, leaning back on her pillow and telling herself how stupid she was being. She was tired. She knew she was tired. She had worked all night, and she had taken aspirin for her headache, which should have helped her to settle off easily to sleep. But for some reason or other, every small noise of the outside world seemed magnified this morning. Even the birds, she thought irritably, seemed to have settled in the trees closest to her windows.

The cigarette which might have helped to soothe her nerves and helped her to relax proved in vain, for the loud voice of whoever it was calling came up to her, muffled though it was by the intervening ceiling.

' Sounds as though Mother has a queer client in this one,' Joy decided, finishing the cigarette and debating whether or not to try once more to settle down or to put on a dressing gown and find out for herself just what was happening, when her mind was made up for her. Aileen, who was normally the most gentle-voiced member of the somewhat noisy family, was answering her ' client ', and even muffled as it was, to Joy her mother's voice sounded distressed and in a state of emotional upset.

' I'm going down to find out what's wrong! ' Joy's mind was made up on the instant. Aileen had shouldered too long the burdens of normal family living entirely alone, the burdens normally shared between a husband and wife. Whenever she could, since she had grown old enough to realize the responsibilities which faced her mother and which had faced her ever since the day of the accident to her father and to Pete's parents, Joy had stepped in and taken whatever she could of the load from her mother's shoulders. Now, without pausing to think of the rest she was missing, rest which had so far eluded her completely, she pulled on her slippers and dressing gown and went swiftly and silently down to the old morning-room which Aileen had made her own office.

Joy tapped on the door, but did not wait to be bidden to enter. She pushed the door open, her glance going immediately to Aileen's face. Her mother was still seated at her desk, but her usual pretty colour was missing, save for two bright spots of angry crimson which touched her high cheekbones and the added light in her eyes which made them seem suddenly too bright, as though she were holding back the tears.

'Is there anything I can do to help, Mother?' she asked quietly. 'It sounds very much as though there's something wrong.'

'Oh, dear!' Aileen's distressed glance flew back to the man who was firmly planted in front of her desk. 'Has . . . have we wakened you, darling?' she asked anxiously. 'I did try to tell Mr Bainbridge here . . .'

'Samuel Bainbridge, miss, representing the Vanmouth Incorporated Development Trust,' he announced pompously. 'I take it you're Sister Benyon, of St Lucy's Hospital? Your lady mother here'—he turned and smiled at Aileen, and abruptly Joy was astonished at the change in his expression and almost had to pinch herself to make quite certain she was not dreaming— 'tells me there's no man of the house and that I must talk to you about my proposition.'

'What proposition?' Joy demanded, feeling distinctly at a disadvantage in her long dark blue dressing gown and flat slippers. As though she could read her daughter's thoughts, Aileen rose to her feet and brought forward two chairs, pushing one towards Mr Bainbridge with a smart prod from the toe of her shoes.

'Sit down, darling,' she invited, adding in a somewhat cooler tone of voice: 'Won't you take a seat, Mr Bainbridge?'

Samuel Bainbridge seemed unaware of anything at all adverse in the atmosphere. He settled himself in the chair, crossed his legs and brought out a slim gold cigarette case and proffered it first to Aileen, who murmured 'Not just now, thank you,' and then to Joy, who shook her head. 'I've just put one out, thank you,' she told him.

'Good round!' he commented, smiling. 'Can't say it ever works out like that at home *or* at the club! Never mind, maybe you'll both join me some other time? Now, about this proposition, Miss Benyon. I may as well tell you right at the start you'll never get another one half so good. . . .'

'Perhaps not,' Joy agreed calmly, 'but you'll first have to tell me just what this is all about . . . what your proposition is, as an instance, won't you?'

'I'm a business man, Sister Benyon,' Mr Bainbridge began. 'I can't tell a story of "from rags to riches" or any romantic nonsense of that sort, because it just wouldn't be true. My father, rest his soul, left me what he considered comfortably off. I agreed with him—up to a point—but standards have changed a great deal since he died, and what seemed a comfortable income just after the war isn't such a comfortable one these days. There I'm sure you'll agree.'

He looked from Joy to her mother and back again as though awaiting confirmation of his observations, but as neither of them spoke he waited a moment or so and then continued.

'I made a bit of extra money during the war years,' he announced complacently, 'and since then I've managed to make a bit more. It's amazing,' he said as though making some wonderful discovery and announcing it to the world, 'how money seems to attract money, if you know what I mean?'

Still neither mother nor daughter offered a comment, and as the silence lengthened Joy felt an unaccountable satisfaction in the fact that Samuel Bainbridge was obviously beginning to feel a little uncomfortable.

'Serves him right,' was the thought—totally alien to her usual good nature—which crossed her mind. 'Coming in here and making all that noise, whatever it is he wants! I wish he'd hurry up and come to the point and have done with it!'

'I've spent two or three summer holidays abroad,' he continued after a time. 'Last year we stayed in what was called on the brochure "a holiday village". It was good fun. Like a holiday camp only more extensive. Everything was catered for in and around a small section of the coastline. Sands, amusements, restaurants, music, dancing, a casino, kiddies' corner, bathing pools, walks for the young lovers—the lot. You name it, that village has it. I'd thought of starting the same thing here in Vanmouth. Lots of people don't want to go abroad for their holidays. Some of them have pets they don't want to board out. Some of them have relatives they can't take with them for illness or other reasons, and yet don't want to leave in hospital or a home. I've got a few business friends together, men like myself who can contribute financially as well as in a material way, and we've had the plans passed and everything. It only needs . . .'

He paused so long this time that Joy, who was suddenly beginning to feel very tired, decided to help him out:

'Needs what, Mr Bainbridge?' she enquired. 'I don't really see where Mother's business bureau comes into this! I should imagine your best idea would be to get some good secretarial staff of your own and have everything on the premises, so to speak.'

'That's just the idea.' He beamed upon her as though glad he had encountered someone who appeared to be talking his line of common sense. 'But it wasn't secretarial work I was thinking of,' he continued, 'not at the moment, although there'll be plenty of *that* in the near future. No,' he heaved a big sigh, took out another cigarette and lit it from the stub of the other one, 'it's this house and the ground that goes with it.'

'This house? And the garden?' Joy knew she must sound stupid, but that was the effect this man was having upon her, probably, she thought, because of her extreme tiredness and the aspirin combined.

89

'Mr Bainbridge,' Aileen said gently, 'is willing to meet any reasonable offer you may name for this property, Joy. He wishes to use the house as a residence for his staff . . . I think that's what he said, and the grounds for . . . I've forgotten what.'

'A garden for the use of the staff only, with an enclosure for sun-bathing and that sort of thing,' Samuel Bainbridge expounded. 'It's a regular sun-trap here, just on this corner. We should have our own private road made to the beach, of course. . . .'

'Mr Bainbridge,' Joy rose to her full height, forgetful now of the dressing gown, the slippers and the fact that she had entirely cleaned her face of make-up before she went to bed, 'I must inform you that you're wasting your time.'

'I don't think so,' he smiled blandly. 'Your mother, begging your pardon, Mrs Benyon'—he beamed cheerfully on the speechless Aileen—'wouldn't even listen to anything I had to say. All she would tell me was that it had nothing whatsoever to do with her, and that I must wait until you'd done whatever you're doing at present—night duty, I think she said it was—and then have a chat with you. I'm prepared to match any figure you name, Sister Benyon, within reason, that is.'

'I'm afraid you still haven't got the picture, Mr Bainbridge.' Joy kept a firm hold on her temper and the tone of her voice was well controlled. 'This house and garden are not for sale, to you or to anyone else, either now or in the foreseeable future.'

'You don't appear to understand, Sister Benyon,' he said stubbornly. 'You and your family can have a house just as roomy as this and more modern in design, in the new part of Vanmouth, down at the end of the bay where we've built the pleasure gardens.'

'We happen to like Fernbank and everything about it. Its design, its position, its amenities, the garden, everything. We are not interested in moving.'

'I don't know anything about your affairs,' Sam Bainbridge said slowly, 'but I have heard you have a sister who isn't . . . very well. I don't know what's wrong with her or anything about it, but I do know Doctor Moyser is here every day. With what you get from the Vanmouth Development Trust,' he said magnanimously, ' you could afford to take her to the best doctors in the world who specialize in whatever she has wrong with her.'

' My sister is being taken care of by Doctor Moyser and the other people from St Lucy's, thank you, Mr Bainbridge,' Joy said firmly. ' There's already a very marked improvement in her state of health since we came to live here, and I'm certain it will not be long before she's completely well once more.'

' I'm glad to hear it.' The words were sincere, but he was beginning to look grim. Joy knew without being told that he was accustomed to everyone he met being so impressed by the Bainbridge money, however much it might be, and the trust he represented and that he did not like to be thwarted. ' Is that your last word, Sister?' he asked very quietly.

' I'm afraid so.' Joy looked steadily at him, willing him to go, but he cast a last appealing glance in Aileen's direction before returning to the attack.

' Then listen to me, just a moment, young woman,' he began. ' If I start out to, I can make things very difficult for you. I don't want to do that . . . for your mother's sake.' Again that glance at Aileen, but she sat quiet and still, not responding. ' But if you drive me to it, I'll fight!'

' I can see nothing in what you say to make me change my mind,' Joy said firmly, but she was beginning to tremble slightly. The way in which this man persisted in looking at her mother was beginning to alarm her. Aileen was still an attractive woman. She had kept her youthful figure, though sometimes Joy had wondered whether her mother's slenderness, which might have been envied by many a girl half her age, was the result of all the miles she had walked over the years to save bus fares, the plain and scant meals she vowed she enjoyed, to save expense! Whatever the reason, Aileen was slender and lithesome, her face in spite of all the worries and cares she had carried alone for such a long time, was still almost free of lines and wrinkles. Her eyes and her hair were attractive, and she still had all her own teeth which showed prettily white when she smiled. Altogether Aileen was an attractive woman in the prime of life, and Samuel Bainbridge was showing his appreciation of the fact in a manner which left Joy in little doubt as to his thoughts.

'You will do,' he said menacingly, taking out his cigarette case again and proffering it almost, it seemed, automatically, but both mother and daughter shook their heads. 'Just listen to me for a few minutes,' he invited, 'and then see if you wouldn't like to sing a rather different tune!'

CHAPTER X

'My business partner has managed to buy the land adjoining your house and garden,' Samuel Bainbridge told them, articulating each word with such emphasis that they could not possibly misunderstand. 'We shall build as closely to your property as we possibly can, but,' he held up an admonitory finger, 'we shall *not* build a staff residence, because I feel sure, before the project is completed, that you'll see how useless and unbusinesslike it is to refuse my offer.'

'What you choose to do with the adjoining land—or with anything else, for that matter—is of no consequence so far as I'm concerned,' Joy announced relentlessly. 'I would like to explain something to you, Mr Bainbridge, if you have still a few minutes to spare.'

'Go ahead,' he answered cheerfully. 'I'm a reasonable man, as I've already explained to your mother. I'll listen to anything within reason.'

'This house,' Joy was annoyed to find her voice trembling a little as she thought of Miss Barnes and her entrusting her 'dearest possession' to herself, 'its contents and the grounds surrounding it, were entrusted to me in the will of the late Miss Muriel Barnes. She did not wish the further development of Vanmouth, or so I understand.'

'She and a few more like her,' he agreed quickly enough. 'They're none of them young enough to appreciate the quick, modern way of living. They still think of the place as it was when their grandfathers or fathers built their big, often ugly old houses here. They don't think of the youngsters of today, those who want their pleasures while they're still young enough to enjoy them. They don't want the little ones to have their fill of fresh air and sea breezes, not if it means sacrificing a bit of their precious old town.'

'I hardly think that's fair, Mr Bainbridge.' Joy drew a deep breath as she interrupted his flow of words. 'I

93

walked along the front two or three days ago, and there were lots of children, paddling, bathing, building sand-castles. Their parents were relaxing, letting the beach patrols take care of the children's safety. The town appears to have catered very well indeed for its visitors, and so far as I could see they were apparently a well satisfied crowd.'

'Maybe, maybe, for those who've been coming here year after year since they were children themselves and don't want to see changes made any more than do the old stagers still living here. We want to attract the young folks, the new parents. . . .'

'Those with big wages and money to spend, eh, Mr Bainbridge? That's what you're thinking about, isn't it?' Joy asked, waving a protesting hand as he began to speak again. 'Just a minute, please,' she urged. 'I haven't quite finished. I have nothing whatsoever against any plans you may have to brighten the town and to augment its facilities, although when the twins asked me to help them find somewhere to go the other evening the problem was rather which place to chose than where to find one! You appear to have three good cinemas, a live theatre, and an open-air show twice each week of the season. There are two bathing pools, one, I understand, used only by children, which I think is a wonderful idea. No,' she shook her head until her curly mop, unrestricted by her Sister's cap, danced about her ears, 'I really don't see the necessity for all this fuss about a holiday village, when you obviously have enough board-ing houses and private landladies, to say nothing of hotels, where your visitors can be accommodated.'

'They still have to spend money on entertainment,' Samuel Bainbridge said angrily. 'Our idea is every-thing in one little part of the town—it won't detract from any other business, either the boating lake or anything else. The council would never have passed the plans if they had thought that might be the result. No, it's the young parents, the courting couples I want to see here.'

'But I'm afraid you'll have to look elsewhere for living quarters for your staff, Mr Bainbridge,' Joy said

94

firmly. ' I gave my promise to Miss Barnes that I would look after her interests.' A faint smile touched the corners of her mouth as she remembered the moment, then was gone . . . gone as Miss Barnes had gone, she thought, remembering swiftly. ' That I intend to do. I'm sure she wouldn't have sold out to you.'

' She could have done.' He let the words slip out and then obviously and immediately regretting them, added: ' If she'd lived long enough, that is.'

' Did you offer to buy the house in her lifetime, Mr Bainbridge?' Joy asked directly, and he had the grace to look a little uncomfortable.

' Yes,' he said briefly, ' that's why I thought it might be possible to buy it, after she'd . . . now she's gone.'

' Then I'm afraid you've made a mistake.' Joy turned to go back to bed, but somehow she did not want to leave this man with her mother. Aileen got so agitated when people shouted, and obviously Samuel Bainbridge was accustomed to shouting when things were not going the way he wanted them to go! ' I gave my word,' she insisted, ' and apart from the fact of what this house means to us as a family, I should never go back on a promise made to a dying woman,' she ended softly.

' Poppycock!' If Joy had not felt so upset and so serious about this menace to their happiness she knew she would have laughed in his face. He looked so very outraged. ' A promise made to anyone in that state should never be considered binding,' he asserted. ' If it is then it's a form of emotional blackmail. How could you know that one day someone would come along and offer you maybe three times the value of the house and land, because it happened to be just what he wanted? You can't tell me a promise should be kept in the face of something so advantageous to all of you as that?'

' I can and I do,' Joy said firmly. ' I gave my word, and Miss Barnes trusted me to keep it, as I intend to do. And now '—she smiled brightly and opened the door as an added hint—' if you will forgive me I must get some rest, and I know my mother has a great deal of work planned for today. . . .'

Reluctantly, and with a last, lingering glance in Aileen's direction, he got to his feet and allowed himself to be shown through the door and conducted to the hallway.

'You haven't heard the last of me, young lady,' he said in ringing tones as he stood on the step. 'I'm always prepared to fight for what I want. And I'm warning you now, now we're out of the earshot of your dear mother, who appears to be a far more reasonable person than you'll ever be, I fight with any weapons I can lay my hands upon, all the time!'

Joy watched him go roaring away down the shore road in an obviously new and opulent car which her recently acquired interest in such matters told her was a super Mercedes, then she turned and went slowly back to where Aileen sat, chin cupped in her hands, staring into space.

'Nice individual,' commented Joy with a touch of sarcasm, something she seldom used. 'What did you think of him, darling?'

'I felt sorry for him,' was the unexpected answer, and Joy knew she must have registered her surprise in her face as her mother turned fully towards her, frowning slightly.

'Why, for goodness' sake?' Joy felt the question to be perfectly justified. She could not, at the moment, see any reason whatsoever to be sorry for such a self-important man as Samuel Bainbridge appeared to be.

'I'm sorry for anyone who believes that money can purchase anything—or anyone—on the face of the earth,' Aileen said quietly. 'I know the old joke about " money can't buy happiness, but at least it makes it possible to be miserable in comfort ", but that's not the whole of it by a long chalk. It can buy books, but not brains. It can buy the best food in the world, the most expensive, but what good is that if a person, for some reason, hasn't an appetite? It can buy a house but not always a home, and that's what I seem to feel Mr Bainbridge lacks, whatever else he possesses.'

'I suppose you could say it could buy a pew in church —or it could at one time—but not a place in heaven!

Just as it can buy a bed to sleep in, and the softest of sheets and pillows, but there are many sufferers of insomnia who would like to purchase sleep! I'm not one of them, thank goodness, though early this morning I was beginning to feel I might be! I think he'll have gone about his business now, whatever it is and wherever he goes to conduct it, but when I heard him shouting I just had to come and see what it was all about.'

Aileen smiled but made no further comment, and when Joy left her and went back to bed her mother was already fitting paper and carbons into the new electric typewriter she had just purchased, and for her another day's work had begun.

Joy expected to lie awake worrying about their recent visitor, but to her surprise she fell asleep almost at once and did not waken until Sylvia tapped on the door and brought in a cup of tea, saying it was time to dress and go back on duty.

'You should see the gorgeous flowers Mum's had sent,' she told Joy as she perched on the end of her sister's bed, her shining cap of sleek chestnut hair bobbing with excitement. 'Simply out of this world!'

'Who's sent them?' Joy asked idly. 'Doctor Quentin?' for Quentin had turned up at Fernbank on more than one occasion with a sheaf of freshly cut flowers from his mother's garden, for Celia was an ardent gardener and co-operated with the man who attended to theirs by her own clever skill in the choice of flowers guaranteed to give the most exotic blooms.

'No.' Sylvia shook her head until her long, almost shoulder-length hair swung like a bell around her small, pointed face. 'A man who called this morning. Must have been about some typing he wanted doing or something. Anyhow, seems Mother's made a conquest. You should just see them!'

'They aren't from somebody called Bainbridge, by any chance, are they?' Joy challenged.

'How did you guess? You must have known something,' Sylvia said accusingly. 'That isn't fair. You didn't say anything to me. There was a card with them. It said "with apologies for my disturbing you this morning. S. Bainbridge". That was all,' she ended in a tone of hurt disappointment.

'And quite enough, too,' Joy said shortly, inwardly more disturbed than she would allow her sister to guess. 'Run along now, poppet, and run my bath for me, please. I'm going to be late if I'm not careful.'

'Jenny Wren'—that was Sylvia's name for Mrs Wrenshaw ever since she had discovered that lady had an initial J in her name—' says you didn't get much sleep this morning, Joy. Was something the matter? Had it anything to do with this Mr Bainbridge, whoever he is?'

'Something like that. Now, scat!' Joy waved her arms in a mock threat, and laughing, Sylvia ran away to do her sister's bidding, but there was no laughter in Joy's eyes or in her heart as she had her usual quick, refreshing bath and prepared to go to St Lucy's.

'I must make some enquiries about him,' she told herself as Nigel sounded his horn outside and she hurried out to meet him, but she shrank from making enquiries from Nurse Byecroft, Nigel or anyone she had only recently met. She did not want their affairs to become the talk of either the hospital or the town.

'Quentin will know all about him,' she consoled herself. 'It's one of his nights on Casualty. If I can get down there before I go on duty I might get the chance of a word or two.'

As it happened there was a lull in the casualty block when she went down. Quentin greeted her with the sort of smile she still could not make up her mind was reserved for his favoured friends or distributed to all and sundry.

'Care for a cup of tea, Sister Benyon?' he greeted her. 'Nurse here has just made a fresh brew.'

'Yes, please.' Joy smiled at the girl, who trotted off to the kitchen, as Joy had expected she would, to produce the required beverage. As soon as they were alone Joy turned to Quentin.

'Do you know a man called Bainbridge, Quentin?' she asked. 'Samuel Bainbridge. A big, well-set-up man physically, iron grey hair, and a thick thatch of it. Wears expensive clothes—they look like Savile Row tailoring to me, what little I know about such things—and drives an enormous, brand-new Mercedes car?'

'Yes,' Quentin said briefly, 'I know Sam quite well. A nice enough chap—if everything's going his way—and a bad one to cross if things aren't going the way he wants them to go. Why?'

It did not take long to give him a brief outline of the morning visit of Samuel Bainbridge to Fernbank, and of the subject of their conversation. She mentioned the gift of flowers as a finale, indignation oozing from every pore.

'That sounds most unlike him, I must say,' was Quentin's comment. 'He's as tough a nut as you could meet in a month of Sundays, and that's not under-estimating him! Your mother must have made quite an impression on him. But beware of him, Joy. He likes his own way, and he has the dickens of a temper. Dad's his doctor, and I know he's treating him for heart trouble, but I'm not sure what form it takes. I know he shouldn't get as excited as he does, but I suppose that's the way he's made. All the same '—he gave her an anxious glance—' you need your sleep in the day, remember. If you like I'll ask Dad to have a word with him.'

'I'm all right, thank you,' Joy assured him, and indeed at the moment she felt fine. 'This is one of the times I'm glad I was trained with discipline. It makes one respond to duty, to normal working hours and demands, even if one feels fit to drop, even if one has worries or anything else. It simply doesn't occur to one to . . . give in.'

'No.' Quentin gave her a long, cool stare which, for some unknown reason, brought the colour into her cheeks. 'It *never* occurs to you to give in, does it, Joy? Anyone else of your age, faced with so much responsibility as you've had these last years, would have "given in" long ago. I admire you,' he said very softly. 'You just aren't the giving in sort!'

Fortunately, Joy felt, she was spared the necessity of a reply as the nurse came back with the cup of strong, sweet tea favoured by most of the staff when on duty. Then two boys arrived, carrying a third and younger boy who had fallen down the cliff. Joy left the casualty department to its own devices, and went back to her own ward, but as she went out Quentin hurried after her.

'Don't let old Sam get you down,' he advised. 'His bark's worse than his bite, I think. Anyhow, since his wife died, about ten years ago, he's had little to occupy his mind but building up his moneybags into an even greater pile. Bound to have narrowed his outlet somewhat, even though he has a family, I think he more or less leaves them to their own devices, providing they toe his particular line. If he gives you any more trouble let me know and I'll see if I can do anything to help. The kids are nice enough, what little I've seen of them, so he can't be all that difficult to deal with unless he's out adding another corner to his own little empire!'

Joy thanked him and hurried away, but there was a little warm glow in her heart which had not been there before. Crumbs from her rich—emotion-wise—sister's table, she thought wryly, but at least she felt better for having told Quentin what had happened and for his understanding.

There were no further immediate difficulties where Sam Bainbridge and his affairs were concerned. Before the end of the week he had sent round a vast pile of work for Aileen, with a request that it be 'completed as soon as possible, please'. Aileen worked almost all night, but the job was done, and done perfectly. The next morning she went round to the labour exchange and engaged a copy typist and to the office equipment showrooms and ordered another typewriter. If he came with another order like that last one she was going to be prepared! But when Joy protested that she did not want her mother to work like that, Aileen merely laughed.

'He may be testing us or something,' she said gaily. 'Let him send all the work he likes. I'll cope. But he'll have to pay and pay well for it, especially if he wants work done in a hurry!'

'Why not let him have the house and charge him double what he offers?' Lana asked suddenly. 'You could set up a trust fund of your own then, for the Wrenshaws, Cousin Emma and all of us, and we could find somewhere else, I'm certain.'

'I'm not going back on my promise,' Joy said firmly, 'and '—her face softened as she saw how much better Lana was looking these days—'you don't really mean that, you know, darling. You wouldn't like me to betray the trust old Miss Barnes put in me, would you? I just couldn't, and you wouldn't really like me to.'

'I suppose not.' Lana smiled in return, holding out her arms and suddenly enveloping the willing Joy within them, a Joy who felt a surge of delight sweep over her as she realized how much stronger was Lana's grip these days. 'It just wouldn't be *you*,' Lana finished softly, 'and when all's said and done, I think you're the most wonderful sister in the world!'

'Go along with you,' Joy said, laughing, but she was pleased all the same. Appreciation from the lovely Lana had been a rare thing for some time past, now, it seemed, with a regaining of a little strength, something of her old generous and happy spirit seemed to be returning too.

It did indeed appear that any further trouble from Sam Bainbridge had been shelved, at least for the time being. There were signs of activity from the other side of the high hedge, and Lana, who spent so much of her time lying out in the garden, reported a high wooden fence being erected just on the other side of their trees. There were varying noises of lorries unloading, of hammering and loud voices of men hard at work, then suddenly one morning, a new sound greeted their ears just as Joy returned from St Lucy's.

'What is it?' Emma demanded of Joy as soon as she entered the house. 'It started at half past seven and it hasn't stopped since.'

'It's a pneumatic drill,' Rex said knowledgeably. 'More than one. They've started on that part of the road which runs right down to the shore, right across what we used to think of as the waste land.'

' There's more than one,' Sylvia added. ' I watched them unload. You can see right across from the attic windows.'

Joy tightened her lips. If this was Sam Bainbridge's way of trying to annoy them she was going to do her best to defeat him. She wasn't sure as yet what she *could* do, if anything, but surely there was no real necessity to suffer this kind of thing after a night on duty on the wards?

Turn the problem over in her mind as often as she might she was still no nearer an answer as, later than usual, she went up to her room and prepared to try and get some rest, but outside, despite the windows being closed and the air in the room growing more and more stuffy as the morning wore on, the noise continued, until at last she got up, pulled on her dressing gown and slippers and went out into the garden to see whether or not the annoyance was affecting Lana as well.

CHAPTER XI

'It is rather much,' Lana said in reply to Joy's enquiry about the effects of the noise from the adjacent plot which, if anything, seemed to have increased in volume during the past half hour. 'I suppose they have to use these things when they're taking up roads and so on, but I rather fancy that's not quite what they *are* doing.'

'Well, whatever it is it's a dreadful, nerve-racking row,' Joy said emphatically. 'Just what *do* you think they're doing, if they aren't ripping up the road?'

'Breaking up that rocky stuff they want to have level to build their chalets or whatever they call their little summer-time houses on,' Lana said briefly. 'Emma climbed on that kitchen step-stool yesterday and had a look. She was very satisfied they would have great difficulty in getting their drains and foundations and things in, but it doesn't seem they're going to have much difficulty after all. *We* are, if this goes on!'

'How right you are!' Joy gave a sharp sigh for her own fast vanishing rest period. She was back on duty tonight, but, thank goodness, tomorrow was one of her two nights off. Tomorrow, she vowed, she would certainly make up for what she missed today . . . but in the meantime she had to consider that she had still two further weeks of night duty to face.

'Wonder how Mum's making out,' she managed above the noise. 'Maybe it doesn't sound so loudly in her office. I'll go and see.' But when she went in to Aileen she was greeted, most unusually, by a frown and a sharp request to 'hurry and close the door, dear, please. It helps to deaden the sound.'

Aileen looked pale and headachey, and the temperature of the room told its own story. Until this morning she had been working with the windows wide open to the sounds and scents of summer. Now the windows, as well as the door, were tightly closed and although Aileen seldom smoked Joy could detect the smell of stale tobacco in the air.

'Poor darling,' she thought sympathetically. 'She must have been in quite a state to resort to smoking! And Cousin Emma, rheumatic twinges and the lot, climbing on to a stool to try and see just what was going on!'

'Don't worry about me,' Aileen smiled suddenly. 'I had a bright idea and put cotton wool in my ears. It's helped a lot, but it makes it difficult to hear the phone, and I have to take it out when I'm talking to anyone, and for some reason or other lots of people seem to have chosen this morning to ring up. Must be that small advert I put in the local paper. Anyhow, it's all good for business, the telephone calls, I mean. And this noise can't go on for much longer. They're bound to get to a quieter phase of work before long.'

'I read somewhere, or saw it on some news programme on the television or something'—Joy wrinkled her brow as she strove to recall just what she had seen and where, but the thought eluded her—'that there had been some sort of machines or compressors developed which didn't make any noise at all. They've even been used in roads adjoining hospitals. Surely, if Mr Bainbridge and his friends have as much money as he said they have, then they can afford some of the very latest equipment?'

'Maybe they can, maybe they don't even know about it, but that's hardly likely,' Aileen observed. 'I should think he just hopes we'll object enough to want to move out!'

'Then he's in for a great surprise,' Joy announced with renewed determination as, abruptly, the sound increased again in volume and Emma tapped on the door to report that a lorry had just delivered a *third* machine, which had been put into immediate operation. Sylvia had seen it taken off the lorry from her vantage point at the attic window.

'That settles it.' Joy pulled the cord of her gown about her as though, Aileen thought whimsically, she

were girding on armour! 'I'm going round there . . .
at once! One machine would be quite adequate for
what they have to do, even if it would take them longer
to do it! They couldn't have their precious holiday
village completed, advertised *and* booked up for this
season, anyhow, so I don't see that there's any necessity
for all this racket!'

'Joy!' Aileen protested, but without much real hope
of achieving anything. She knew her daughter in this
mood. 'I don't think it will do very much good! There
will only be workmen there, and they'll be acting under
orders. It isn't fair to blame them for whatever instructions Mr Bainbridge or one of his co-members of the
Trust has told them is to be done.'

'There's bound to be someone in charge,' Joy said
insistently, 'a Clerk of Works, a foreman or *someone*.
He's the one I hope to see now. I'll deal with Mr Bainbridge later, wherever he lives or is to be found.'

'I'd rather you didn't . . .' Aileen began, but Joy
laid a gentle hand on her mother's shoulder.

'Don't worry so much, darling,' she advised. 'I
hear Mr B. is quite a nice chap, if everything's going
his way! Well, it's high time he accepted the fact that
there are other people in this world as well as Samuel
Bainbridge, and that they don't all happen to be de-
pendent upon him for their bread and butter! I shan't
quarrel with him—even if he's there—unless he opens
hostilities in my direction first. But I have to think
of my rest, your work, Lana's health—this noise *must*
be getting on her nerves, lying out there in the garden
and so close to it all. And I really can't have Emma
or Jenny Wren climbing up and down to find out what
it's all about! One or the other of them might fall and
break a limb! Then we'll have a second helpless person
in the family!'

She did not wait for any further protests Aileen might
have to offer. Instead she dropped a light kiss on top
of her mother's head, then left the room, running up
to dress as speedily as she could.

It did not take many minutes to change, apply a

light touch of make-up, and prepare to do battle, as she phrased it to herself. She had put on a shift dress of deep blue crease-resistant linen, brushed her hair until it gleamed and danced about her head, touched her generous mouth with lipstick and decided she was ready.

'Let's hope he's an understanding sort of foreman or boss or whatever he's called!' she whispered to her image, then she ran lightly downstairs and out through the front door, going the short distance to the rough track the lorries had already made over the waste land next door.

She stood for a moment, startled by what she saw. There were high piles of timber, what appeared to be masses of bricks, plastic and glass sheeting, ladders, wheelbarrows, spades and shovels, a huge concrete mixer and all the general paraphernalia of a building site. Over in the far corner, not very far from the Fernbank hedge, was one of several newly erected wooden huts, but this one bore a sign on a board near the door: Clerk of Works.

Close to where Joy stood, slightly bewildered by all the activity around her, a man shut off the pneumatic drill he was working and grinned at her.

'Looking for someone, miss?' he asked her. 'Maybe I can help you?'

'I want to see whoever is in charge here, please,' Joy said, summoning back her courage now it had actually come to the point. To be strictly truthful, she had not been too sure of this idea of hers, the bearding of the lion in his own den, as it were, even when she had told her mother so emphatically that that was where she was going, but the man to whom she had spoken seemed sympathetic enough. Still grinning all over his weather-tanned face, he pointed one finger at the lettered board.

'I expect it's Mr Michael you want to see really,' he said, 'he's in there. But I'd hurry up if I were you, miss. Mr Sam'll be back any time, and he isn't one to have social calls on the site!'

'This isn't exactly a social call,' Joy told him, wondering who on earth 'Mr Michael' might be. Probably one or another of his co-members of the Trust, she decided, and, picking her way over the littered ground, she went to the door of the small hut and knocked as loudly as she dared.

'Come in!' The shout from inside was barely audible, and after a moment of further hesitation she turned the knob and opened the door. A young man was sitting on a high stool at a shelf under the window, which apparently served him as a desk with the light coming in above it. He turned as she entered, an exclamation which had sprung to his lips dying unspoken. When he saw who his visitor was he took off the horn-rimmed glasses he was wearing, revealing a pair of startlingly clear grey eyes, and advanced the pace or so permitted by the small space to stand before her.

'What a pleasant surprise!' he astonished Joy by his first words. 'I'm very sorry,' he went on apologetically, 'but this site won't be completed and open before next season, and that's only if things get a move on now, before the autumn starts . . . that is '—he broke off and gave her the benefit of a charming smile—'I'm assuming that you've called to enquire about booking one of our chalets or accommodation of some description?'

'I'm afraid not,' Joy said crisply, and since she could not address him as 'Mr Michael' without knowing at least who he was, and since she had no idea what his full name might be or what he was doing there at all, she looked up enquiringly. 'I'm afraid I don't know your name,' she apologized, 'but I'm from Fernbank'—she jerked her head in the direction of the fence and hedge—'next door. I really came to ask if it's necessary to make *quite* such a noise in the pursuit of whatever it is you're trying to do. *One* of your many machines would be more than enough to keep me awake—I'm on night duty for this week and a further two weeks—at St Lucy's Hospital. In addition I have a sister who is somewhat incapacitated, and whose only pleasure is to lie out there, in the garden, a pleasure completely destroyed, I might add, since your men got to work this morning.'

'It is rather too much, I agree,' he smiled unexpectedly. 'I don't suppose my father gave it a thought when he left his instructions with the foreman. By the way, I'm Michael Bainbridge, and this is my first job as a civil engineer,' he ended. 'I'll see what can be done.'

'I'm Joy Benyon.' They shook hands solemnly. 'I have met your father,' she added, not knowing how much Sam Bainbridge might or might not have said about herself and her refusal to sell to him. Michael laughed. He had, she discovered, a rather pleasant laugh, but he seemed somehow as though that particular exercise was one in which he did not indulge very often.

'You'll be Sister Joy Benyon, then.' Michael smiled as she nodded. 'I've heard about you,' was his only comment, but he took her by the elbow and began to escort her from the site. 'My father has one of those new drills,' he explained, 'only just out in this country, and it's practically noiseless. I know, because it's just been used in the vicinity of a hospital we've been building up in the North. I'll see what can be done about getting it or one like it down here by tomorrow. The Plant Equipment Hire people may have one they can let us have. In the meantime'—again the charming smile—'there's lots of digging and so forth these chaps can be getting along with.'

'Thank you,' Joy said gratefully, annoyed because she felt somehow a little deflated by the fact that there had been such a sudden and generous acceptance of her complaint. 'I'll be getting back, then.'

'You catch up on your rest if you can, Sister,' Michael advised. 'People who do your sort of work need their rest when they're due for it!'

They parted with cordial exchanges on both sides, and Joy went back into the kitchen to explain the sudden cessation of noise which had disappeared as though by magic.

'Mr Michael's not long been qualified,' Jenny Wrenshaw said from where she was washing salad ready for lunch. 'He's a civil engineer or something. Anyhow, he's got a degree to his name, which is more than his dad'll ever get, for all his cleverness!'

'It takes all sorts to make a world,' Joy smiled, 'and I'm only too thankful Mr Michael didn't exactly take after his father! He was most kind and considerate.'

'They both are,' Jenny affirmed, 'both him and his sister. But Sam's made them do what he decided, ever since their mother died. I always thought young Miss Cara would follow her mother's footsteps. She was a lovely woman, and clever too. She used to do what she called "create hats", and some lovely things she made in her time, that I will say.'

'And what does—Cara, did you say? What does *she* do?' Joy asked curiously.

'Nothing.' Jenny's jaw set. 'Miss Muriel used to talk to her sometimes, when they met in the library. Miss Cara wanted to go to London, something in advertising, I think it was. But her dad said there was no need for her ever to worry about earning a living, and that she'd better concentrate on finding herself a man . . . but Miss Cara never seemed to bother with boys. She was always trying to help people instead. Did some work for Oxfam, some for some youth organization or other and went abroad for a bit, and came back full of all sorts of plans and schemes about devoting the rest of her life to people less fortunate than herself, but her father soon put a stop to *that*!'

'How?' Joy was interested in spite of herself. She was wondering just what it must be like to have a father such as Sam Bainbridge and lack any means of opposing him, since he appeared to control the lives of his family and in some ways—maybe only where this Cara was concerned—seen to it there were no qualifications which would enable her to leave home and to lead a life of her own.

'She'd been to what he called a "finishing school" and all that sort of thing,' Jenny said with some scorn, 'but that would only have helped her if he'd set her up in a hat shop of her own, as she wanted him to do, and he wouldn't. No '—she tossed the washed salad in a bowl as she spoke—' he sent off Ella Wilkinson, who'd been his housekeeper for some years. Gave her a small cottage and a pension, just enough to keep body and soul together, and packed her off. He lets Cara go up to see her every now and then for what he calls a holiday, but it's really so that she can keep an eye on Ella and make certain she's not augmenting her income in any way, letting a room or growing something to sell or anything of that sort. Ever since then Miss Cara's lived at home and kept house for her father, poor kid.'

' I wouldn't,' Joy announced decisively. ' I'd do something! Anyhow, that's not *our* worry, thank goodness. I feel we've coped with our present problem, at any rate for a time, thanks be!'

It certainly seemed that way. The noise of the drills and the bumper had ceased since her visit, and although there were sounds of activity from the other side of the fence, they were not unduly loud or in any way unbearable. Joy went to see first her mother and then Lana, and was congratulated by both on the success of her visit, then she went back to her room and undressed again, slipping back into bed and was soon sound asleep.

She was wakened from her slumbers by the renewed sounds of the drills and mixer going at full strength again in the plot next door. It was impossible to get off to sleep a second time, and after a while she got up. bathed and dressed and went out to Lana, who said wearily that her head was aching and that Joy's visit hadn't really done much good after all.

' This will be because Sam's come back,' Joy decided. ' He's the one I'll have to tackle, and I will. Just let me get a strong, hot cuppa to bolster my courage, and I'll go round and tell him exactly what I think of him.'

She was as good as her word, but this time she made an effort to look as businesslike and as efficient as possible. There was no hesitation in her step this time as she picked her way carefully across to the door of the little hut, watched, she knew, by the eyes of more than one of the workmen.

As though by magic the noise had ceased as she walked across the site, and when she knocked on the door she could clearly hear the voice which called 'come in', but she almost stood where she was, rooted to the spot by the sound of that voice. It was not the voice of Sam or of his son, but that of a girl, and when Joy pushed open the door she found herself confronted by a small, slight girl of about nineteen with brown hair cut with a fringe and hanging to her shoulders, something after the style of Sylvia's.

'Hello.' The girl held out her hand, a slim, well-shaped hand with the long, spatulate-tipped fingers Joy would have expected. 'I'm Cara Bainbridge. Michael told me all about you. Sorry about all the racket all over again, but when Dad came and found Michael had sent for different gear he was furious. That won't stop the stuff arriving, though, but I think he's hoping to make you give in before it comes. I wouldn't '—she grinned suddenly—'because you have something of your own . . . something to hold on to, to fight for, and if I were you, I'd fight!'

'That's just what I intend to do,' Joy said, liking the girl as much as she had liked the brother. Their mother, she thought abruptly, must have been a very sweet person. Sam, too, might have been more pleasant when his wife had been alive! 'You can give your father a message for me if you will,' she added. 'Tell him there's some sort of law about noise abatement. I don't know how it operates, but I'll find out. I shall go to the police station tomorrow, when I come off duty. And if I have to prosecute in order to get a good sleep then I will. Will you tell him that?'

'Good for you!' Cara said unexpectedly. 'Of course I'll tell him, and I think he'll back down. He likes to keep on the right side of the law in every way! He's not a bad sort when you get to know him,' she laughed lightly. 'He just likes all his own way, and he usually gets it. It might do him a world of good to find there's someone he can't order around and get away with it!'

'Thanks.' Joy found herself suddenly liking the girl

more than she would have believed possible. 'Why don't you come round and meet my sister some time?' she invited. 'I think you two would have a great deal in common.'

'I'd love to.' Cara's words were sincere. 'Mike *said* you were a lovely person.'

'Sometimes.' Joy felt the betraying colour in her cheeks at the unexpected compliment. 'I'm afraid your father wouldn't agree!'

'He'll be all right, once he's got what he wants in and around this precious village of his,' Cara opined, 'but take my advice. . . . Don't let him beat you down!'

'I won't!' Joy joined in her laughter. 'See you at Fernbank some time, then,' she called as she said goodbye.

The noise from the building site continued all afternoon, but Joy could do nothing more about it. She would wait until the morning, she decided, then, if the noiseless equipment hadn't arrived, or if Sam Bainbridge wasn't prepared to meet her halfway, she would carry out her threat and go to the police station and see what help they could give.

She was almost ready to go on duty when there was a ring at the bell, and a moment or so later a flustered Jenny Wren came into the lounge where she was collecting up her things ready to leave and where she and Lana had sought refuge all afternoon.

'There's a young gentleman called, Miss Joy,' she announced in an agitated fashion. 'I'd have taken him in to your mother, but it was you he asked to see. It's Mr Michael Bainbridge.'

CHAPTER XII

As Joy hesitated, Lana appeared to suddenly awaken
to the fact that someone, an attractive stranger whom
she had heard about only that day, was at the door,
asking permission to enter.

'Ask him in, Joy,' she urged from her couch. 'I'd
like to see something of this Bainbridge crowd for myself. You get out and about, and you've seen them all!
I only hear what you tell me!'

'But I'm going on duty in a few minutes,' Joy protested. 'Mrs Wrenshaw can tell him to call some other
time.'

'I want to talk to him . . . *please!*' Lana urged.
'You don't know how fed up I've been all day, all
that noise and Mother working, the twins out at this
holiday job or whatever it is they've found for themselves, and you asleep. . . .'

Joy knew it would be useless to mention the Wrenshaws or Cousin Emma, since each of them had been
busy in and about the house all day. A place this size,
and all these people and furniture in it, took a deal of
keeping up to, Jenny was fond of saying, and Emma,
who was by no means as active as she used to be, had
entirely agreed, helping wherever and however she could,
which did not leave her much time to spend beside
Lana's couch as in the old days.

'There's the Wrenshaws and Emma here to keep an
eye on the proprieties, if that's what you're worrying
about,' Lana went on. 'And Mother isn't very far
away.'

'I wasn't worrying,' Joy assured her truthfully.
'Very well, then. But I can only stay a minute or so.
You'll have to entertain him yourself after that. And
make certain he doesn't stay too long and tire you out!'
She nodded to Jenny, who hurried away to return a
moment or so later with a smiling, fresh-faced Michael in
tow. Joy performed the introductions, seeing as she saw

so often when people met Lana for the first time the struggle between admiration of her beauty and the pity for her condition taking place in Michael's expression.

' I had to come round and apologize.' He spoke to Joy, but his glance went back almost at once to Lana, as though drawn there by a strong but invisible magnet. ' Dad was furious, as Cara says she told you. But when she told him what you said about going to the police, he said he would see to it personally that the other hired equipment was there in the morning, so I don't think you'll have any further need to worry. I hope not, anyhow.'

' I hope you're right,' Joy said agreeably. ' If you aren't then I shall have no alternative but to go round to the police station and ask for help. And now '—she glanced at her watch—' if you'll excuse me I must be off. I'll just fetch my bag and gloves from upstairs.'

One or the other of them made some response, but in such a low tone that it was quite impossible to hear what was said. They were already talking together, with an animation on Lana's lovely face which had not been there since the day her accident had happened, and Michael, it seemed, was hanging on to her every word.

' Poor Quentin!' Joy thought as she banged her drawers shut with quite unnecessary vigour. ' It isn't enough for this Michael to be a good-looking young man, and to have an attractive personality—and there's no denying that he has just that—he also has to have the money, or the expectation of it, that Lana wants from the man she marries. I only hope Quentin isn't going to be hurt.'

It never occurred to think that she, Joy, was the most likely person to be hurt out of all of them. Her only thought was for the man to whom she had felt herself drawn even at their first moment of meeting. She was certain he was in love with Lana. Who could see her, get to know her, even a little, and not love her? she asked her image as she settled her hat on her head.

' And Quentin has done so much for her already!' she though as she ran downstairs and popped her head in to say goodbye to her sister. Neither Lana nor Michael seemed aware of her presence until she spoke a second time. When Lana looked up, it was with a new radiance in her face, a new light in her eyes. She smiled in a bemused fashion in her sister's direction, fingering some coloured snapshots which lay on her knees.

'Michael's been showing me some photographs he took on his last holiday in Greece,' she told her sister. 'Do you think . . . I'd like to go there, one day,' she ended softly.

'There's no reason why you shouldn't, if you really want to,' Michael said before Joy had opportunity to speak. 'This'—he gestured towards the rug which covered her from the waist downwards—'is incidental . . . if you *really* want to go, that is.'

'It's an impossible dream,' said Lana, so low that Joy only just caught the words, but there was no mistake about hearing Michael's reply.

'Nothing is impossible,' he said firmly, 'not if you want it enough, believe in the rightness of it enough. Try for it, work for it . . . wish for it, pray for it, if you like, but you have to do your own bit towards whatever it is you're after. . . .'

Joy did not stay to hear any more. She would be late on duty if the friend with whom she was to travel tonight had already gone, but the other nurse was waiting, and as they drove together up the hill to St Lucy's, even as she chatted of this and that to her companion, Joy was wondering all the time about this new relationship which had entered so abruptly into their lives.

'As if coming to Vanmouth wasn't enough of an upheaval and change in itself,' she thought as she went into the Sisters' room and prepared to take over her ward for the night, 'we have to become involved with this Bainbridge family, and somehow or other, much as I like the son and daughter, I'm afraid we haven't heard the last of father Sam and all his ideas!'

There was not time to think or worry further about Sam or his family and their concerns that night. There were two births during the small hours of the morning, and another mother-to-be was rushed in just before Joy came off duty, already in labour, and the birth would be premature. One way and another she was glad when it was time to return to Fernbank, time to go up to her own small room again and to sleep, secure in the knowledge that for her a night free of duty lay ahead.

There were other things to think of, however, in the days which followed. Michael had been quite right when he had told them his father would attend personally to the delivery of the new and almost silent equipment, and for the household of Fernbank all seemed well again. Except, that was, from Joy's point of view. Sam Bainbridge continued to send or, more often, to bring in more and more work for Aileen's flying fingers to cope with. As she laughingly remarked to Joy one afternoon when the night duty weeks were approaching their ending, ' He brought as much in for his firm, Trust or whatever they call themselves as I had from all my other clients put together.'

' I don't like it,' Joy confessed. ' I don't like feeling we're doing anything for that man.'

' That's not a very logical outlook, darling, and not in the least like yourself!' Aileen chided. ' He pays for what I do for him, and he's always said how good the work is . . . which is more than Mr Fordyce ever said in all the years I worked for him! And really, apart from this '' thing '' he has about wanting Fernbank, he's not such a bad sort of person when one gets to know him,' she said gently. ' I think he's rather lonely.'

' If he is it's because he's too bad-tempered and wants too much of his own way to ever keep a friend,' Joy said briefly. ' And '—her glance went to the enormous sheaf of gladioli Sam had brought round with him that morning, although he knew they had plenty of flowers in their own garden, and from there to his gift of grapes fresh from his own vine—' I don't like the way in which he's trying to get round you to persuade me to do what he wants! I shall never break my word to Miss

Barnes,' she said fiercely. ' I wish he could understand that.'

' I think he does understand and admires you—secretly—for sticking to your guns, as he phrased it only the other day. He can't give in, or at least I suppose he thinks he can't give in, not with a reputation such as he has of always getting his own way in the end, now you've taken such a definite stand against him. But I don't think he's trying to " get round me " as you put it, because he knows—for I've told him—that in matters such as this, where the promise you made was such a personal matter—I abide by your decision.'

' Then you'll let him see we don't need his work, or his money, won't you, Mum?' Joy asked, feeling suddenly sorry for Aileen, for the woman who had worked so hard for so long, without a man by her side, missing so many of the pleasures which would have been hers had the children's father lived.

' But I advertised for this work, Joy.' Aileen sounded so woebegone and so miserable that Joy was instantly contrite. ' I have absolutely no reason to refuse his business requests,' she ended, half defensively, and impulsively Joy crossed to where Aileen was seated behind her desk and gave her a spontaneous hug.

' I know you haven't, darling,' she said quickly, ' and I'm sorry I tried to interfere. I won't again,' she promised rashly, ' not unless you ask me to do so.'

' I'm asking you to do so right now, Joy,' Aileen surprised her by the statement. ' I'd like your advice. Sam . . . Mr Bainbridge . . . has asked me to have dinner with him at the Silver Dolphin,' she named the largest and most expensive hotel in the town. ' He says he would like to talk to me out of business hours. He's booked seats at the theatre for the same night, too. There's a London company coming down.'

Joy hesitated a moment, wondering what this might portend, and suddenly she knew, as though it had all been revealed on a screen and set up for her to absorb the information, of all the lonely hours Aileen must have spent since their father died. When Joy was away during her training, and Lana engrossed in the fashion world which she had graced for so short a time, the twins too young for companionship, and Pete engrossed either in his studies or one or the other of the absorbing hobbies which he enjoyed to the full. Cousin Emma was a sweet person, amiable to live with, but in no sense a companion for a woman of Aileen's quicksilver nature and alert, businesslike brain. It must be wonderful to meet a man of her own age or thereabouts, who could talk about the things she best remembered and had enjoyed, who too had known what it was like to lose his partner and face the world with children of his own to bring up single-handed. She smiled into Aileen's anxious eyes.

'If you want to go, darling,' she advised, 'then go. And I hope you enjoy yourself. But mind now'—she raised a mockingly warning finger and her eyes twinkled despite the severity of her words—'you're not to allow him to bully you into anything you don't want to do or into going anywhere you don't really want to go. You don't *have* to be polite to him, remember,' she stressed. 'He's neither your employer or the landlord!'

'I know, darling,' Aileen agreed, laughing with her, but there was a hint of tears behind the laughter and when she spoke again her voice trembled despite her efforts to control it, 'but there's something I like about him . . . although I'm hanged if I know what it is.'

'Must be something I haven't spotted yet,' Joy laughed again good-naturedly, 'but I'll back your character judgement any day of the week, so off you go, and enjoy yourself with my blessing. Seems we'll have to get accustomed to a lot of new ideas now we're living in Vanmouth. Did you know Cousin Emma has joined the Townswomen's Guild?'

But there were more 'new ideas' to which they had to grow accustomed as the days went by, Joy discovered. Quentin still paid his daily visit, although he now seemed to spend a great deal more time with the family in general, taking a hand in all manner of household activities which astonished Joy, from the discussion on the colour scheme being planned throughout the house to Wrenshaw's idea of a goldfish pond in the garden. The twins consulted him on every point, and when Joy protested that his time was too valuable to be expended in this fashion, she was faced by two pairs of wide, innocent eyes and mouths which were guiltless of that mischievous quirk for which she instinctively looked when she suspected them of pulling her leg.

'He told us to count him in as "one of us", Joy, honestly,' Rex said. 'He says he likes being part of our family. It's fun.'

Fun it might be, Joy reflected as she lay back in a sun chair on the lawn thinking over all these matters on one of her free afternoons, but it was all extremely emotionally wearing.

Lana was undoubtedly making progress. Whether this was due to the various vitamin tablets and potions with which Quentin had insisted he was 'building up her lowered resistance . . . her metabolism's all to pot ', or whether it was that the prolonged visits of Amy Calvin and Hugh Tate were beginning to take effect, or whether —here Joy's thoughts sheered off at a tangent and became chaotic—it was because Michael Bainbridge never missed a day either, but that some part of it saw him comfortably installed at Fernbank, either out in the garden with Lana or in a chair pulled up beside her couch if she happened to be indoors, Joy could not have told. The fact remained that progress *was* undoubtedly being made, but so far Quentin had not broached the subject of the outpatients' clinic to Joy or to anyone else in the family. He and Lana appeared to share a secret, and watching her sister, first with Quentin and then with Michael, Joy began to worry about which of them was the more likely to be hurt, and much as she liked Michael, she hoped with all her heart that it was he and not Quentin who would be told his love was unwelcome.

A shadow fell across the book which lay, opened but unread, on her lap. She looked up to see Michael looking down at her, his white shirt open at the throat, his eyes laughing as usual as he dropped on to the grass beside her chair.

'Permission to bring another person into your little family circle, Sister?' he asked, pulling at the grass. 'I've just had a word with Lana, and she said not to bother your mother but to ask you.'

'Who is it?' Joy asked, sitting upright and closing her book. 'Anyone we know?'

'Not yet, but I hope you'll get to know her *and* to like her,' Michael said seriously. 'Her name's Beryl Lowe, and she's the daughter of Dad's partner. All his life—or at least since he and Bill Lowe went into partnership together—they've planned and hoped Beryl and I would marry. I like Beryl, she's a nice girl, and I know she likes me, but there's nothing more to what we feel for each other than just that, though neither of our fathers will see it that way. Beryl's an only child, and she's more than a little lonely. Her parents would wrap her in cotton wool, if they thought they could keep her with them, just as she is, for ever and ever. They know that's impossible, so they think the next best thing is for me to take over where they've left off, but although we like each other that's the last thing either Beryl or I want to happen, and she's so starved for a little decent female company I've told her all about you and the family here, and . . .'

'Bring her along,' Joy broke in, laughing. 'I declare, you must have some Irish blood in your veins, Michael, the way you manage to persuade folks to agree to almost anything you suggest! Anyway,' she concluded, the laughter vanishing as she rose, 'if she belongs to a family like that they're sure to live on Valley Road, and maybe we'll seem a rough, harum-scarum lot if you do bring her here! The twins are a little boisterous at times, and Cousin Emma's . . .'

'A darling,' Michael interjected. 'You're all darlings, every one of you! And Beryl'll love coming to a real live bustling family where she'll be sure of a welcome.'

Real, live and bustling the family might be, Joy reflected as she went indoors in time to hear the telephone in the hall ringing but no one hurrying to answer, but there never seemed to be anyone around when she most needed them! Mrs Wrenshaw was down at the bottom end of the garden picking blackcurrants for a pie. Wrenshaw was staking his chrysanthemums. Lana could not get to the phone, the twins were out somewhere on business of their own, and Aileen could be dimly heard pounding away on the almost silent electric typewriter. Her calls were switched through to her now, on the extension telephone they had installed, and Joy fully expected that this would be yet another client to add to Aileen's already very full list.

It was with a sense of real surprise and, she was amazed to discover, of genuine pleasure, that she heard Pete's voice at the other end of the line.

'May I come down for the day tomorrow, Joy?' he asked after they had greeted each other. 'Don't worry about my . . . bothering you again. I won't. I just wanted to see how everyone is and to follow up a hint I've had from that solicitor friend of yours, Mr Belding. Seems I may have the chance of a good job in Vanmouth if I pass whatever test they set.'

Joy told him they would all be delighted to see him, asked questions about the job, but he said he would show her the letter when he arrived and they would 'have a family pow-wow as we've always done'. She said they would be able to put him up for the weekend, and they parted with assurances on both sides that the weekend ahead should be an interesting and delightful change, and as she hung up, before she went to tell her mother and Jenny there would be an extra person for a few days, she realized how pleased she was going to be to see Pete again, someone who wasn't part of this emotional mix-up which had seemed to grow around them since they first moved into Fernbank.

CHAPTER XIII

Joy was thankful she was back on day duty once more with all the promised activities which lay ahead where her family were concerned. August was drawing to its close, and the twins were full of stories gathered from a variety of sources in and about the town, of the new Technical College which they would begin to attend in September, and of the hopes and dreams they believed would be fulfilled through its staff and administration.

She came home at eight-thirty that evening, to find a message by the telephone to say that Pete had called earlier in the day and said he would be along later that evening, but that he had an appointment to keep first and did not know what time he would be free.

In the garden Lana was lying on her couch, her rug over her legs, and as she went out of doors Joy heard the welcome sound of her sister's laughter, and despite her tiredness her heart lifted in thankfulness. How wonderful of Miss Barnes to leave them this house and garden and the wherewithal to enjoy its amenities! How wonderful it was to have a doctor like Quentin Moyser, and two people like Amy Calvin and Hugh Tate to help along the good work! Small wonder Lana was showing improvement day by day, and as she crossed the lawn to where she could see a strange girl seated in the low garden chair by Lana's couch, Joy breathed a silent prayer that the promise of this moment should one day be fulfilled, and Lana be walking, running and enjoying life with the rest of them, just as she used to do.

'Even if it means she and . . . Quentin will go out of my life together,' Joy thought sadly, but as she drew up a chair for herself she knew she did not regret one moment or one incident that had gone since she first knew Fernbank was to be their home.

'I told you about Beryl, Joy, remember?' Michael was smiling as he performed the introductions. 'She was shy at first, but I don't think it will take her very long to get used to you all.'

'I'm sure it won't.' Joy took an instant liking to the tall, well-made girl with the sleek brown hair, the widely spaced dark grey eyes and the sensitive mouth. 'I'm glad they've all been looking after you!'

'They couldn't have been more kind or made me more welcome, no matter who I'd been,' Beryl told her, smiling round. 'I feel I belong already.'

'That's just as it should be,' Joy said cheerfully. 'Where's Mother?'

'Still working. She had some important papers she wanted to get off by tonight's mail. She wouldn't leave any of them until the morning. It's her night on the town with her would-be boy-friend over the fence,' Sylvia said flippantly, but Joy, knowing her young sister, knew this was the girl's way of disguising how she felt about the proposed outing with Sam Bainbridge.

'If Mother wishes to go then I'm all in favour,' she astounded them all by saying, and even Michael looked astonished. 'She's had precious little fun, bringing the lot of us up without any help from anyone, and when all's said and done, none of us is really a companion to her, much as we might try to be.'

'I know what you mean,' Michael said slowly. 'I feel the same way about Dad. I know there's nothing wrong in our feeling this way. It's just that we belong to two different generations, and we don't always remember it. Neither do parents. Our outlooks are so different, our values so changed.'

The discussion might have gone on for a long time, but at that point the back door opened and Pete was giving his old call, just as he had been in the habit of giving it when he had returned to the house in Cranberry Terrace.

'I did telephone earlier.' He had crossed at once to Joy's side. 'Someone, Mrs Wrenshaw, I think, took the message. I hope you . . .'

He broke off, his sentence unfinished, and as Joy looked up at him to see what was the cause of the sudden silence she saw he was gazing at Beryl Lowe as though not certain his eyesight was all right. Beryl was staring back at him, a slow, painful colour rising in her cheeks and mantling her throat. Joy looked from one to the other, quite bewildered.

'I . . . do you two know each other?' she demanded as neither appeared to be able to speak properly.

'I . . . we've met,' Pete managed, and suddenly his old familiar smile was back on his lips and in his eyes, and Joy knew it was going to be all right whatever the cause of Beryl's present apparent distress. 'This is the young lady I told you I'd met the day we came to Vanmouth Court,' he went on, adding to the mystification of everyone save Joy and Beryl, 'the one with the little pup on the end of a very long ribbon. Remember?'

'I certainly do.' Beryl's eyes were shining and although the high colour in her cheeks had died down there was still a look of rosy contentment as she smiled up at him. 'I'd never have caught Sing-Yen that day if you hadn't acted so promptly.' She paused for a moment, then added: 'Did my father get in touch with you? I told him about you and he said he'd maybe be able to help.'

'If your father is Mr Lowe, then I've just left him and I start work with some Trust with which he's associated, the week after next,' Pete told them. 'He was very pleasant.'

'He can be,' Beryl said briefly, glancing at Michael as though for confirmation, 'but, like Michael's father, he's used to having all his own way!'

'I got along all right with him, anyhow,' Pete announced, 'but from what I gather he doesn't come into that side of affairs very much.'

There was a general discussion in which introductions sorted themselves out as Michael, Beryl and Lana tried to make Pete see the position of the Benyon family where the Trust was concerned. Tiring of a conversation which could obviously get them nowhere at the moment, Joy excused herself and went back into the house to see how much longer her mother intended to work. Quentin was just coming into the hall via the front door as she went through. He looked tired, she thought. He touched her arm, delaying her as she would have passed him and gone straight to her mother's room. She had found it better, these last weeks, to keep out of Quentin's way. Somehow it hurt too much to see him with Lana. Although she told herself it was because she did not want to stand by and see him hurt if Lana turned eventually, as she appeared to be doing gradually but surely, to Michael, the young man with so much money and such wonderful prospects in the fullness of time, she knew the truth was that she herself was beginning to discover for herself how painful unrequited love can be.

'What ward are you on now, Joy?' he startled her by his next question.

'Women's Medical,' she told him. 'Why?'

'Because the two cases I sent in yesterday might very well turn out to be poliomyelitis,' he said soberly. 'I wasn't sure at first, but Dad says he's certain now the symptoms are developing. We're sending them up to the fever hospital at Maryhill, and the three men who were admitted on Saturday. I don't want to be pessimistic, but we may very well have a scare on our hands.'

'What's being done?'

'Well, we're fixing up centres, of course, for vaccination and distribution of the "sugar lump" vaccine. That's under way already. We're taking samples of every patient reported in the area, save for something simple like a broken arm or leg,' he smiled, 'but you get the general picture.'

'I do indeed,' Joy nodded. 'How long since there was any sort of general vaccination of the public in Vanmouth?'

'Approximately two years ago,' Quentin told her. 'The new mothers, of course, are all advised to take it in the stride of babyhood, and I must admit most of them do. It's the young people who either didn't bother at all or only went part way with the prevention we're worried about. And the older age group, the up to forty-fives. Some of them have queer ideas as to what

125

three drops of vaccine on a homely-looking sugar lump can do to prevent this sort of thing happening. By the way'—again that anxious glance—'what about all of you here? The Benyon family, so to speak?'

'We were all vaccinated or had the requisite dose of sugar two years or so ago,' Joy answered promptly. 'We should be all right.'

'Does that include Lana?' was the next question, and Joy was relieved to be able to nod her head, giving the affirmative.

'Nurse Brown saw to that,' she said. 'They were all most efficient, and I have to hand it to them, they couldn't insist, of course, but they were extremely persuasive!'

'Good.' Quentin straightened his shoulders as though a weight had been lifted from them. 'That takes a load off my mind,' he grinned. 'I really think we're beginning to see some good results where Lana is concerned now. It would be a pity for anything to happen and put her back . . . further than where she was when she came to Vanmouth.'

'It would indeed,' Joy agreed. 'I'll keep an eye on her. Now I must go and stop Mother working. She's going out tonight, and unless I go along she's going to be in one mad, mad rush to get there, and I'm certain it isn't good for her.'

'It most certainly is not,' Quentin agreed. 'Tell her I say so. She works far too hard on this new venture of hers already. Surely it isn't as vital to the family's existence as all that?'

'Not now,' Joy acquiesced. 'But I rather feel she wants to prove something to herself. She's always had this dream of a bureau of her own, and now the dream has come true she *has* to prove it wasn't just a dream but a worthwhile reality. We shouldn't starve,' she smiled faintly, 'even if she went back to a part-time job as a typist or book-keeper somewhere, but I think I understand how she feels, and providing she doesn't overdo things I shan't interfere. She was always a career woman—fortunately for the rest of us—rather than a housewife, but she hasn't made such a bad job of both, in my opinion. Now we have the Wrenshaws, and Cousin Emma's so much better with the sun-ray treatment you've been giving her up at the clinic, I feel it only fair that Mother should have her fling at seeing what she can do to build up the sort of thing she's dreamed of for so long.'

'Well, keep an eye on her, Joy, and on the rest of them too, there's a good girl. And '—again that lovely smile which she would have liked to believe was for her alone but which she was convinced was the face he normally turned to all his patients to encourage them —'make sure you take care of yourself!' he added. 'That's an order!'

'Certainly, Doctor.' Joy smiled in return, bobbing him a mock curtsy, and she did not notice as she walked briskly away that the smile faded from Quentin's eyes as his glance followed her trim figure and that he heaved a sigh before turning to continue making his way out to the others.

'I simply can't understand Joy,' he had told his mother only the previous evening. 'She . . . that night we first met, when she'd done such a good job with the laddie who'd come a cropper from his bicycle, I could have sworn she felt the same instinctive . . . I don't know how to put it, but the same sense of " belonging " that I told you I felt the moment I set eyes on her. But she seems to avoid being alone with me whenever I go to the house. She never stands to talk or say anything more than the usual things about patients, Lana or the family. It's as though she's erected a wall between us, invisible but still there and completely unscalable.'

'She has had a great deal of responsibility for a long time, dear,' had been Celia's answer. 'I know her mother has done wonders for the family, but she couldn't have done what she has done without her daughter's help, *and* she takes all her responsibilities very seriously indeed. That much was apparent at the very beginning.'

'She still has a right to a life of her own,' Quentin grumbled, ' but she never seems to think about that. I suppose, one day . . .' He had not concluded his sentence, but there had really been no necessity to do so. Celia and her son understood one another very well, and she had known precisely what he meant.

'Yes,' she had said quietly, 'one day . . . maybe before very long now. Just be patient a little while longer. She's a girl worth waiting for!'

He couldn't agree more, Quentin reflected now as he went out to the others, and with an effort he dismissed Joy and his own hopes and dreams to the background of his mind. There would be time for that later, he told himself, once this job, this task he had set himself to accomplish was an accepted fact. In the meantime he wished he had reminded her to see that everyone—herself included—had plenty of rest and did not take their relaxation in the more crowded parts of the town.

Unaware of his concern for her welfare, Joy had gone into her mother's small office where a tired-eyed Aileen was putting the cover on her machine for the day. A neat pile of work ready for the post lay on her desk beside her, and she was just about to stamp the envelopes as Joy opened the door.

'Let me do that.' Joy crossed the room and, as she had expected, found her mother's neat pencil figures of the amount of postage necessary ready on the top right-hand corner of each envelope. 'You hurry along and get ready for your date! Take your time. I shouldn't worry about keeping Mr Samuel Bainbridge cooling his heels for a few minutes. Might do him good!'

Making a wry face at her daughter, Aileen laughed and left the room, knowing she could confidently leave the finishing off, the posting and any tidying up of personal bits and pieces to Joy. What she would have done without the girl in the years gone by Aileen shuddered to think, but her heart was a little heavy as she thought of the near-quarrel between Joy and the man she, Aileen, knew she could grow to love and to trust, the man who, she was aware, had already decided to pursue his 'courtship' of herself, maybe, she reflected abruptly, because in that way he hoped to be able to persuade Joy to change her mind about Fernbank.

'She mustn't,' Aileen whispered to her image in the mirror, 'not even if it means he and I quarrel instead! Joy would feel she had let old Miss Barnes down, and she'd never be happy again. And beside all that, Fernbank has been such a wonderful adventure for all of us . . . given all of us a different outlook, a different way of life!'

She dressed quickly but with unusual care. Even as she applied her light make-up she smiled as she reflected that at her age it seemed a little ridiculous to set out deliberately to make a man give in to what he would surely class as a 'woman's whim'. 'I don't care if he does,' she told herself defiantly. 'I shall try to talk him out of it, tonight and any other time I have the opportunity to do so. How lovely if I could come home tonight and tell Joy it was all over and settled, and that Sam was going to do without Fernbank, that he'd found an alternative way of doing whatever it is he wants to do!'

But it was late when Sam's big car delivered her at the gate of Fernbank. The household was almost in darkness, and as she fitted her key into the lock, signalled to him as he waited at the gate that she was all right, and let herself into the house, Aileen knew she had failed in what she had set out to do. Sam had talked of his 'holiday village', that was true, but nothing would move him from the conviction that Fernbank was needed to complete his plans.

'I've had another part of the bay offered to me,' he had said over dinner. 'Well, not to me exactly, but to a member of the Trust. I don't think you'll know where I mean, but it's the part known locally as Sandside, just beyond the pier. There's a fair-sized hotel with it. Place hasn't been let this year. Its last owners couldn't make it pay, and we could get it at our figure. But . . .' he had banged the table with a large, emphatic hand, 'I've set my heart on Fernbank and that corner. And when Sam Bainbridge sets his heart on anything, he usually gets it!'

Aileen had been about to say something, but there was

a gleam in his eye which told her instinctively that if she were not careful he was prepared to make the matter more personal, and she was by no means ready for that as yet. She had turned the conversation skilfully into other channels, but throughout the evening Sam had hinted in one form or another that he always got what or whom he wanted in the end.

She felt tired as she went into the kitchen. There was a small tray set with her customary glass of milk and three biscuits, and in the wide rocking chair, which Jenny had told them had been in the Barnes family for generations, Joy lay asleep, her head pillowed in her arm as it rested on the table.

Quietly Aileen got a second glass of milk from the fridge and heated them both up, adding more biscuits before she wakened her daughter. Joy lifted her head, shaking herself awake.

'Come along, baby,' Aileen suggested. 'You ought to have been in bed ages ago . . . another time, when you know where I've gone, don't wait up. I've a key, remember, and if I needed you I can always ring now we have a phone of our own!'

Joy was too tired to argue or to protest. They went upstairs side by side and parted at their respective doors, but it was only when she had asked Aileen if she had enjoyed her evening and been told ' it was a wonderful change . . . yes, thank you ' did her earlier words really appear to mean anything.

' Another time. . . .' her mother had said, Joy recalled as she undressed swiftly, set her alarm clock and got into bed. That meant this might become a regular thing, this ' wooing' as Emma referred to it, of her mother by the man who seemed determined to get them out of their home!

' I hope she's strong enough to stand up to him,' Joy thought as she composed herself for sleep. ' He's not an easy man to get along with, and Mother isn't used to having anyone bully her . . . but somehow she seems to like him.' And with a prayer on her lips that in some way not revealed to her at present everything would work out for the best for each of them in the end, Joy fell asleep and did not waken, despite her alarm clock, until Jenny knocked on the bedroom door and brought in a cup of tea, telling her she would have to hurry or she was going to be late on duty.

CHAPTER XIV

The days which followed were some of the busiest Joy had known in her nursing career. Emergency distribution centres were set up in and around the town, and there were so many nurses from the General and from St Lucy's who went along to help cope with the rush of people who suddenly realized they should have taken the advised precaution some time ago.

In the ward there were four new suspects, but only one of them proved to become a confirmed case and was whisked away to the town's isolation hospital, the new centre opened only a year or so ago, on Maryhill, just outside the town.

'Used to be known as the Fever Hospital, the old building they knocked down there before they built the new one,' Jenny told them one morning as she whisked round the house with the fly-killing spray, convinced as she was that flies were amongst the main carriers of all such germs and virus. 'Used to take all chickenpox and such-like up there when I was a girl,' she went on. 'Very seldom we hear of things like we used to have being serious enough to be hospital cases. Lots of those old diseases appear to have been wiped out.'

'They *could* come back, you know,' Joy warned, 'if people don't take the precautions against disease which science has made available. There are inoculations, vaccines, all sorts of preventatives nowadays that were unheard-of when you were a girl.'

'Took a couple of wars, no doubt, to bring some of these wonders about.' Jenny put away her Aerosol and began to polish with vigour. 'There's a great deal more emphasis laid on hygiene and cleanliness in general now, as well,' she went on. 'I don't just mean in people themselves, but where public health's concerned, all these food inspectors, all these public washing places . . . everything's giving people a better chance these days. I can't understand why it isn't made a compulsory thing to have everyone vaccinated with all the different things as they're discovered . . . that would surely help to fight disease?'

'Of course it would,' Joy agreed, 'and to a certain extent I couldn't agree with you more. But one doesn't do that sort of thing in this country.'

'Folks have to have all sorts of inoculations and vaccinations when they go on a holiday abroad or to a job in almost every other country in the world!' Jenny refused to discard her point. 'I don't see why it couldn't be done.'

'It would be something like compulsory military service in the last war,' Joy offered, racking her brains to remember what she had been told or had read on the subject. 'There were all sorts of exemptions and exceptions, all sorts of loopholes . . . and I suppose there would have to be to please everybody in a scheme of this sort. And if there are loopholes of any kind then the thing can never be a complete success story, at least that's my opinion. But we're a free-speaking nation, and to compel any such thing would be classed as an infringement of liberty or something, I'm sure. Anyhow,' she laughed, smothered a yawn, 'I'm tired. I feel guilty taking my half day this week, when everything's at sixes and sevens, so to speak, but Matron's insisting that those people who are working split turns on duty take all the time off due to them.'

'Quite right, too,' Jenny opined. 'You all deserve a medal the way everyone's worked this week, whatever part they play in the whole of the Health Service. I take my hat off to all of you, but I wish you'd have a word with your mother, Miss Joy. She's not looking too well herself these days, and she's working far too hard, keeping up with all this work everyone seems to want in too much of a hurry. Then she's going out night after night with that Sam Bainbridge. I don't know whether he's trying to get her on to his side in this house affair or whether he's given up the idea, but she's as full of cold as she can be. That's too many nights in too hot rooms and coming out into the cool night air; that's my opinion, anyhow,' she added virtuously. ' Whether it's of any value or not I'll leave it.'

Joy managed to soothe Jenny down, but she smiled as she did so, knowing that Mrs Wrenshaw's words were only a means of expressing the concern she felt about each and every one of them. In some strange way, since the Benyons had come to Fernbank, their joys had become those of the Wrenshaws, and their troubles and worries were shouldered or shared as much as possible by the devoted couple. Aileen especially had a warm corner in Jenny's heart. ' Reminds me so much of dear Miss Laura,' she said so often that, over the time they had been in Vanmouth, Joy had begun to feel she knew the other two Miss Barnes as well as she had come to know Miss Muriel.

Jenny was right, however, she thought now as she returned from the little room which was Aileen's office and where the girl she had engaged to help her cope with the unanticipated mound of work which arrived almost daily told her that Aileen had gone to see a man who wanted a special typescript doing of an historical work on which he had been engaged for some time.

Aileen *was* working too hard. She was enjoying herself too, just as Jenny had remarked, and Joy was not at all sure her mother was able to cope with all this extra activity. As if that were not enough, Pete was to return to the fold, as he put it, the following Monday. He had been to see them two or three times since his first visit, and somehow Beryl had always managed to be there. That was all as it should be, so far as Pete and Beryl were concerned, and now they had the Wrenshaws as well as Cousin Emma to help, things domestically were not so hectic. The fact of more space was a help also, but if extra space dispensed with some of the clutter of Cranberry Terrace, it also meant there were more rooms to dust, more furniture and so on to keep tidy, and when Pete came to stay that would mean an additional room which would require care.

The rent and rates being catered for were an undoubted help, but with their transfer—as they hoped if their exam results, due any time now, were satisfactory —to the new Technical College, both Rex and Sylvia would require new clothes which, not being uniforms, tended to be somewhat more expensive. There were additional lighting costs, and, she reflected ruefully, in the winter months they would have fuel bills for Fernbank which would make their modest ones at Cranberry Terrace look nothing at all. There was the insurance and licensing of the little car which Joy had just cashed some of her savings certificates to buy, and cars, she realized, cost petrol, oil and maintenance, even for someone like Pete who always coped with minor repairs himself.

The answer, then, did not lie in trying to persuade Aileen to curtail her business activities, especially when the bureau held every indication of successful further development, but in trying to persuade her to take on someone else to help in addition to the girl she already had. In that way, Joy reasoned, her mother would not have quite the amount of work for herself which she was tackling at present, and would be more able to cope with the sudden social whirl into which she appeared to be indulging with Samuel Bainbridge.

Joy fully intended to talk to her mother along these lines when Aileen came back, but as usual she was in a rush to get work off to the post, to organize her morning and to somehow be ready to leave with Sam when he stationed his car at the end of the Shore Road at seven o'clock that evening.

' Tell me what it is you think I ought to do when I get home, love,' Aileen put her off now by saying. ' Whatever it is I know your advice will be sound enough, it's just that I'm . . . sort of living again as *myself*, after too many years forgetting I was anything but a weekly pay cheque!'

She laughed as she said it, but although there was a smile on Joy's lips there was no laughter in her eyes. She knew only too well what her mother meant, and she knew too that, secretly, she was pleased Aileen had found a suitable male companion in her middle years, someone who was obviously fond of her, able to support her and who was, she was certain, when he had not set his heart on something, a man of personal charm. Otherwise his two children would not be such lovely people! But just now, with his determination to drive her family from the house he coveted, she felt she would have preferred Aileen's choice to have been anyone else save Sam Bainbridge, suitable though he might be in every other way.

She saw Aileen off, then toyed with the idea of taking herself to the cinema. Michael was sitting in his accustomed place beside Lana's couch. The twins had gone to supper with some new friends they had made, and Quentin had already paid his visit for the day. The wave of influenza, due no doubt to the unstable weather which had swept the town, was causing extra work for all the medical population of Vanmouth, but so far, although two more people had been detained as suspected cases, there were no further confirmed cases of the dreaded poliomyelitis which might have led them to believe they were about to experience an epidemic.

' There's an awful lot of this influenza about, though,' Quentin had said. ' Anyone a little below par . . . you know the drill. No violent exercise or exertion. Just advise them to keep out of crowded places, just for a while. And keep out of them yourself, Joy! I get worried about you sometimes. Why not pop up and see Mother this evening? She'd be delighted, and we shall not be in until late. I can run you home.'

She hadn't said either that she would or would not, she remembered now. There were times when she would have loved to talk with Celia Moyser, for a strong friendship had flared between the two women, although Joy's visits to the large, pleasant house had been so infrequent. But tonight she did not want to talk to anyone. She wanted to lose herself instead in something utterly different from her own worries and those of other people. She glanced at the local paper and saw there was the latest Norman Wisdom comedy showing at one of the cinemas in town. She would go along there and forget everything else until the show ended, then she would walk along the front, call at one of the small cafés and have coffee and walk slowly home. She would be in long before her mother, and during her walk she would think out how best to explain that she was only trying to help, not to interfere, in this new life Aileen had made for herself.

She was just ready to leave the house and had told Jenny where she was going in the event of her being needed for any reason, when Beryl arrived. Joy wondered, for a moment, if the girl had chosen the wrong evening, and as she greeted her she pointed out that Pete was not coming to stay until the weekend.

'I know,' Beryl smiled, 'but I've brought someone to see you. She's asked her brother to bring her, but Michael said you must be sick of the Bainbridge family as it is, and told her to write. I've brought Cara,' she opened the door and beckoned to the girl Joy recognized immediately as the one who had been in the wooden site office on the occasion of her second visit.

'We've already met,' she said cordially, opening the door to its fullest extent. ' I seem to remember I invited you round at the time,' she added.

'You did.' Cara followed them into the hall, smiling. She had the same attractive good looks as her brother, Joy reflected, and once more wondered just how much of their father lay behind each pleasant exterior. ' I was coming, too. I've heard such a lot about you all, especially about your sister, Lana, and it was that which helped me make up my mind.'

'She's through in the little room we've turned over to her exclusive use.' Joy was about to show the two girls in, but Cara held up a detaining finger.

' Just a moment, please, Sister Benyon,' she said with an impish grin which told Joy this was the girl who defied her father to join the youth workers overseas, just because she wanted ' to help other people '. ' It's you I've really come to see. I'd like your advice.'

'I'll help if I can,' Joy told her. ' What's the trouble?'

137

'I want to be a nurse,' Cara answered simply. 'I want to be able to help people like your sister. To care for those like Miss Barnes, the way *you* did. To cope with an accident if I see one, as Doctor Quentin told us you helped that night you first came to Vanmouth. How do I set about it, please, Sister? And how long will it take?'

'Have you any G.C.E. certificates?' Joy enquired. 'It is by no means impossible if you haven't, but they do help.'

'Two English and one maths, all O level, I'm afraid,' Cara said. 'They haven't been enough to do anything for me in any direction which might have appealed,' she ended.

'They'll get you in . . . if you pass a few more things,' Joy said, 'and the first will be your medical examination.'

'I'll be all right there,' Cara was certain on that point. 'I'm absolutely fit, thank heaven. What else?'

'Just a few other little things they'll explain as you go,' Joy told her, 'nothing to worry about. The first thing to do is to get into a hospital. Any thoughts as to where you want to be? Lots of them have their own training schools, or there are larger hospitals where one can do the full course, some even include midwifery, but one generally goes to other hospitals for other courses. I did my midwifery in the north. I did my paediatric and psychiatric in the Midlands. It all depends on what you eventually want to do.'

'I think I'll settle for whatever comprises a good general qualified nurse first and then see,' Cara laughed. 'I hadn't thought any further than that. Really because I didn't know enough about it, I suppose. Where do I go from there?'

'If you want to be local, and want to start as soon as possible, I should write to the Matron at St Lucy's,' Joy advised. 'If you go straight ahead, your training should take three years. . . . Excuse me asking, dear, but how old are you?'

'Nineteen in October,' Cara said promptly. 'That

means, if I work and I'm lucky, I should be able to qualify or whatever you call it by the time I'm twenty-one?'

'You should,' Joy told her. 'And I'd like to congratulate you on your choice of career. It's a wonderful job, and very rewarding. Not, perhaps, as financially rewarding as some jobs we might mention, but there are other things.'

'There are indeed,' Cara agreed. 'Thank you very much, Sister. And now'—she smiled again, and Joy smiled with her—'if I *could* meet your sister? Or are you tired of having the Bainbridge family round your neck? Father seems determined to . . . push his own interests, in all directions'—the impish smile flashed out again—'and Michael almost lives here these days. If you feel you're getting too much of us, just say so, and I'll understand.'

'You're very welcome,' Joy assured her. 'I'll go and make some coffee and bring it in. We'll have a cosy, friendly chat all together,' she suggested, and leaving Beryl to show Cara the way and to make the introductions, she went off to the kitchen where Jenny and her husband were deeply immersed in the adventures of their favourite television serial. Joy waved aside all offers of help and instead made extra coffee for them and for Cousin Emma who had retired to a quiet corner with a book. There were times, she reflected, when to use her hands on one or the other of the few domestic chores left to her by one or the other of these three was a real pleasure, and she carried her laden tray through proudly, only wishing she had known Cara was coming, then she would have made some of the little cakes the family loved so much.

Cara and Michael stayed quite late, until it was obvious Lana was tired and until Cara knew she would have to hurry to prepare the snack her father insisted upon eating, wherever he had been, when he retired for the night. By the time she heard Sam's car at the gate and her mother's key in the door, Joy too was ready for bed, and reluctantly she put off talking to Aileen about her amount of work, worry and sufficient rest until the morrow.

When she went on duty the following morning there was a much more cheerful atmosphere in the air at St Lucy's. Doctor Brindley Parsons, the Medical Officer of Health for the area, was certain now that an epidemic was no longer even a remote possibility, and although they were all tired, and although the authorities were determined not to relax their precautions and vigilance as yet and were urging all visitors to take the 'sugar-lump vaccine' if they had not already done so, there was the general feeling that this time, as so often before since so much had been done to help, the bogey had been defeated.

She was just returning from the second dinner break when she saw Sister Leigh in the corridor. Angela Leigh was a pleasant woman, and she had twice visited Fernbank with typing her sister required done for her. She stopped now, looking into Joy's face with a strangely troubled expression.

' I . . . I'm sorry to be the one to break this news, Sister Benyon,' she said hesitantly, ' but I think you would rather be told. They've just brought your mother into Lucy's. Apparently she felt ill in the night, but didn't want to disturb anyone. We only know this because Lana heard her about upstairs, long after everyone else was asleep. She wouldn't let anyone tell you this morning.'

' She called out as I tapped on her door,' Joy remembered. ' She said not to come in for a moment, that she was late . . . and so was I. I didn't go back.'

' She collapsed after you'd gone. It seems she was forcing herself along by sheer effort of will power to make certain she didn't upset any of you.'

' Well?'

' Mrs Wrenshaw telephoned Doctor Quentin. It's he who has sent her in.'

Joy thanked her, hurried along to her own ward and saw that everything was under control, then she telephoned Matron. As she had anticipated, Matron was most helpful, and Joy was shortly on her way to Aileen's bedside.

Aileen lay on her bed, her chart showing an alarming rise in temperature, her prostration indicating the severity of the toxaemia of the attack. She was flushed, and although she had been given drugs to combat the severity of the pain in her limbs and back, it was obvious she was far from pain-free. Joy felt her heart contract, but as she bent over her mother, she knew, as the nurse beside the bed told her a swab was already on its way for testing, that everything possible was being done, and that it only remained to hope and pray that, bad though this might be, it was nothing more deadly than the influenza which could be combated far more easily than the infection Joy feared she might have caught from one or other of her many contacts from all walks of life.

CHAPTER XV

Aileen's illness lasted a good two weeks before Quentin told them to prepare for her return to Fernbank, but in that time a great deal had happened, a great deal which might have upset her mother had she known about it at the time, Joy reflected.

To begin with, Aileen had *not* the dreaded illness they had all feared, but she had apparently been worrying herself silently and feverishly about the disagreement between her daughter and the man she had made a friend. Joy had known little of this, although she had guessed quite a lot, but once the fever of her illness had her in its grip, Aileen became delirious, and as Joy had begged permission to take part in the specialling of her mother, she heard much which Aileen would never have permitted to leave her lips had she been well and aware of what she was saying.

' It isn't fair. . . .' Joy had to stoop to catch the whispered words from Aileen's parched throat. ' Joy gave her word. Sam oughtn't to ask her to break it . . . not my Joy . . . she's a *good* child. I can't marry you, Sam, not and have you do this to my Joy . . . that's what she's always been, my Joy. . . .'

There was much more. The chief worry in Aileen's mind was, as Joy had suspected, connected with Sam Bainbridge and his insistence on demanding possession of Fernbank. But it had been something of a shock to learn he must already have proposed to Aileen . . . proposed and been refused! It was an even greater shock when, a little later, Joy heard her mother say: ' I do love you, Sam . . . I *think* I do . . . but I've loved Joy a lot longer. She's still my baby.'

Tears were on her cheeks as she looked up to see Quentin's father beside her. He had taken Aileen's wrist in his hand and was taking her pulse again.

' You'll be glad to know,' he told the anxious girl, ' that the swab was clear. This is a case of nervous influenza agitated by extreme nervous exhaustion. She's been worrying about her private problems too long and without confiding in anyone! A great mistake.' He shook out two small white tablets and passed them to Joy. 'Give her these,' he said, 'and I think she'll rest. Once the fever's broken she'll be all right, but I think she ought to stay here a week or so.'

'I quite agree,' Joy said in heartfelt tones. 'And when she does come home I shall take care there isn't any more of this bottling up of her emotions to spare the feelings of the rest of us! It's only since we came to Fernbank to live,' she burst forth impulsively. 'She's never thought of keeping worries and so on to herself before. We've always *shared* problems, ever since I was old enough to understand why she was sometimes so worried and upset.'

'But this time'—Lionel Moyser's tone was gentle and tender as he looked gravely at the overwrought girl beside him—'she had a problem which she felt would only occasion you extra distress. I don't know quite what advice I ought to give you, Joy. Would you care for me to have a word with Sam Bainbridge for you?' he invited.

'No. No, thank you, Mr Moyser.' Joy made up her mind on the instant. 'This is something I must tackle for myself. I shall go and see him when I go off duty and tell him I refuse to have Mother worried and upset in this way. He *must* see that she would be as distressed as I would be myself, if I broke the trust Miss Barnes placed in me. She wanted me to have Fernbank, be-cause, I think, she suspected something like this might happen, and that someone to whom the money was of greater value than the house and its associations, the view and the seclusion of that part of the bay which she loved so much, might be constrained upon to sell out to him, to the Trust or whatever it is.'

'Miss Barnes *did* know.' Lionel surprised her by the statement. 'Everyone who reads the local news knows. There just wasn't anyone of her own family left except one second cousin or something of her late father's, and he's way off in Australia, and by all accounts doing well enough for himself and likely to stay there. He won't have any memories of this country, anyhow, and Fernbank will mean nothing more to him than just a name. That was why, I should imagine, she left the place and her beliefs and hopes in *your* hands, Sister. I think she had implicit faith you would follow her wishes.'

'And I will.' Joy's resolve strengthened as she thought of Miss Barnes. Surely even Samuel Bainbridge would see she couldn't go back on her promise to the little old lady who had placed such faith and trust in her?

Lionel looked at the woman on the bed and back to the girl by his side. Celia had told him how their son felt about Sister Benyon, and with all his heart Lionel approved of Quentin's choice. There appeared to be only one problem so far as he could see things, and that was how Joy herself felt, and she was not giving her emotions away, not in the very least! There were times, he reflected, when stern discipline and iron self-control were things to envy, and also times when it might be better to 'let down one's guard'. But there was no point in pursuing that line of thought at the moment! He touched Joy gently on the arm.

'That's the bell,' he reminded her. 'Officially you are off duty. I give you my word your mother is going to be all right, and I'll leave word with the nurse on duty here for the night to give both myself and you a phone call should she not sleep now.'

'Thank you.' He was reminding her, Joy knew, that she must not overstep her privilege, and with a last glance at her mother she turned to leave the small side ward as Nurse Brooke came to take over for the night.

She telephoned Sam's home before she left the hospital grounds. Cara answered, and before she heard why Joy was telephoning she had to give her own news. That morning she had received a letter from Matron saying she would be accepted at St Lucy's for training starting the first day of the month, and Cara was full of bubbling enthusiasm. When Joy had congratulated her and explained that her reason for calling now was because she wanted a private interview with Sam, Cara's infectious laughter bubbled forth once more.

'Rather you than me, Joy,' she announced dramatically. 'He's been beside himself with worry, ever since he rang up today and someone told him your mother was ill in hospital. I'm glad she's going to be all right,' she added quickly, hoping Joy would not think her uncaring of the effect Aileen's illness would have had on the family at Fernbank, 'but I'll have to warn you! I think Dad's going to ask your mother to marry him. I don't know if she will. I suppose he has a lot of good points if you know how to handle him, and she certainly seems to bring out the best in him, whatever magic she uses, but that's not the point I'm trying to make. If he wants your mother to go on with this typing bureau thing—and he seems to think it's one of the best ideas there's been in the town for a long time—then he'll either have to get another housekeeper or bring Ella Wilkinson back to cope! He'll have to learn he can't have his cake *and* eat it! He's going to be in all evening, anyhow.' She seemed to have suddenly recalled why Joy had telephoned in the first instance. 'He wanted to go and see your mother, but whoever answered the telephone wouldn't allow him. Told him the visiting days and times and that was all, so he contented himself by sending masses of flowers.'

'I see.' The flowers, Joy realized, would not be put out for Aileen until morning. Time enough then to see whether or not Sam had included a card with them. 'I'm coming off duty now,' she went on. 'I'll just go home and change, maybe have a cup of tea or something, and come straight round. O.K.?'

'If you feel like bearding the lion in his den!' Cara laughed. 'I'm going round to Fernbank. Lana asked me. I take it that's all right?'

'Now we know we aren't in a state of isolation, yes, we'll be delighted to have you,' Joy assured her. 'See you soon, then,' and she hurried away before Nigel Webster, who was running her home that week, left without her.

145

The house seemed strange and unhomely without Aileen's presence. It was true they had not seen much of her since coming to Vanmouth, but the fact that she was always somewhere not far away was usually enough. Now their happiness in the house, in Lana's slowly returning strength, in each other was dimmed and it was an unusually quiet household that Joy left about an hour later to walk briskly along the promenade to Valley Road where most of the larger and more imposing modern houses were situated.

The Mount proved to be the largest and most imposing of all the houses in the vicinity. As she walked up the wide, sweeping drive and saw the numerous rooms, the velvet lawns, the tennis court and small but attractive private swimming pool, Joy's admiration for Cara increased. What a great deal of responsibility to lay on the shoulders of a girl of nineteen, to supervise the care and cleaning of this mansion and the cook and one maid, with the help of the twice-weekly visits of the woman who, as Cara put it, came to ' do the rough '. Small wonder that Ella, whatever she was like, had told Cara more than once she preferred life in the small cottage to which Sam had retired her !

Joy pressed the imposing bell and after a few minutes it was answered by the girl she took to be the Italian maid Cara had said Sam had imported a year or so previously. She listened as Joy stated she wished to see Mr Bainbridge privately, and then, with a slow smile which seemed to hold something of a nameless warning, the girl opened the door and showed Joy into a wide, beautiful hall.

' You will be so good as to wait one moment, please,' she said in careful English, then she went out, leaving Joy alone for a moment or so. She was back before the girl had time to look about her, but even a casual glance showed there were objects—sculptures, paintings, china figures and so forth, which she did not believe to be Sam's unaided choice.

' Either his late wife or his children have had a hand in this,' she decided as she followed the girl, ' or else he's paid a fantastic sum to some famous interior decorator to have the place made what he considers worthy of his standing and prestige!'

There was no time for any further speculation on the matter. The girl tapped on another door and opened it for her, closing it swiftly and silently behind her as soon as she had announced the name Joy had given her, the name which had caused her employer to stare as though he could not believe his ears.

'Cook'll know who she is and why she's here,' the girl told herself, and hurried away to tell Cook the news and to speculate on what had brought such a charming girl to see this fierce Englishman who was her employer, at this hour of the night.

In the booklined room, behind the imposing desk he worked on when at home, Sam Bainbridge smiled to himself. He was certain the nurse had come to capitulate, and even though he thought her mother the most wonderful woman he had met since the death of his wife so many years ago now, he could not help the feeling of triumph which swept over him as he saw Joy standing there. He'd let her down lightly, he decided. After all, she was Aileen's daughter. He would also see to it the family lost nothing by allowing him his own way!

'Sit down, Sister,' he invited, pointing to a chair before his desk. 'Cigarette?'

'If you don't mind,' Joy seldom smoked, but just now she felt the need of the feel of the cigarette in her fingers, 'I'll have one of my own. I'm more used to them.'

He made no comment, but leaned across the desk and held his lighter to the cigarette for her, lighting one for himself from the box before him.

'Well,' he invited as Joy sought for the right words with which to open the conversation, 'have you decided on a figure, Sister Benyon? I hope it won't be too high for me!' He laughed slightly as though the mere idea were preposterous. 'Come on, now,' he urged as she still sat silent. 'That's why you've come, isn't it?'

'No.' The one word seemed to stun him into silence,

and before she lost this small advantage Joy pressed home her point. 'I'm sorry, Mr Bainbridge,' she said formally, 'but I've told you already that I shall never be prepared to sell Fernbank to you or to anyone else. I told you that property was left to me to look after and to preserve, along with a few other obligations. I told you that I had given my promise to Miss Barnes.'

'And I'll tell you again what I told you at the time,' Sam was shouting, but he wasn't aware of it. 'Poppycock! That's what it is. All poppycock. You gave a promise to a dying old woman whose wish was to stand in the way of progress, of modern living conditions. . . .'

'Not in the way of progress, Mr Bainbridge,' Joy corrected him, gently but firmly. 'Miss Barnes and her sisters had already set up a fund to help various causes of research, various societies which aim to control some of the so-called advantages of modern living, but that's beside the point.'

'If you didn't come here to tell me you were willing to sell, then what the blazes *did* you come for?' he thundered at her. 'You didn't come to tell me your mother was ill. I found that out for myself this morning.'

'I came because what I have to say has some connection with Mother's illness.' Joy forced the words out bravely. 'When I was with her, earlier today, she was in a state of delirium. Mr Moyser, Doctor Quentin's father, says she has caught this influenza virus when she was already in a state of nervous exhaustion. During her delirium, Mr Bainbridge, I learned a great deal I ought to have guessed long ago. I learned that you've asked her to marry you, and that she loves you.' It had been even more difficult to say those last few words than she had ever imagined it could be to say anything, but they were out at last, and the man before her looked as though suddenly he had been given a glimpse of heaven. For a moment Joy felt she could almost see the man Aileen must see behind his everyday exterior, but it was only for a moment.

'It was as much a surprise to me as it evidently is to you,' she said quietly, 'but that isn't the point. She

148

has been worrying about this business of the house. She doesn't want me to break my word.'

'If she loves me there's no point in worrying any more about the house, is there?' Sam demanded. 'She'll be mistress here the very day she says the word. The offer to the rest of you still stands, but I can't see that she has any need to worry about that.'

'I don't expect you to,' Joy said simply. 'You're just not made that way. We are, all of us. A promise given is a promise to be kept, and that's all there is to it. You could have built your precious holiday village down by the pier.'

'I happen to want it where we're building now,' Sam interrupted. 'I have my reasons, young woman, and I don't see that they're any concern of yours!'

'What you fail to understand,' Joy's tone was still quiet and even, but Sam was growing more and more agitated every moment, and Joy, knowing the state of his heart, was a little afraid. Because of this she chose her words carefully, speaking slowly and quietly, hoping to calm him down. 'What you fail to understand,' she repeated, 'is that Mother has apparently refused your proposal. Can't you possibly think why, when she let the truth slip out without knowing it, and she admitted she loves you? Why, Mr Bainbridge? Can't you guess?'

'Because you're the one telling her to refuse me,' Sam blustered, but Joy took him up at once.

'I didn't,' she refuted quietly, 'because she hasn't told me—or, more correctly, she isn't aware that she's told me, that you've proposed at all . . . but now that I *know*,' she emphasized, 'I shall certainly do all I can to prevent it, even though I think you would both be happy, because she would never rest if she knew you had driven me into breaking a promise we both hold sacred.'

She had not known what to expect. More fireworks, perhaps, more shouting, more argument. But as though a candle flame had suddenly been blown out, extinguished, the anger died from Sam Bainbridge's face even as she looked at him.

'You win, Sister Benyon . . . for the moment,' he said grimly. 'One of your mother's most attractive qualities is her unswerving loyalty to the family, to all of you. I can't fight that. I won't ever mention buying Fernbank to your mother again, I swear it. But that doesn't mean I'm giving up trying to persuade you to sell.' Unexpectedly he leaned across the desk and held out his hand. 'You keep your point of view and I'll keep mine,' he suggested, 'but if you promise not to interfere between me and your mother, I'll promise never to mention Fernbank again in her hearing, unless she mentions it first. I may be a hard man, a keen business man, but I respect a worthy opponent, and you are just that, Sister Benyon. Will you shake hands on that little bargain, and may the best one win?'

CHAPTER XVI

It did not take Joy long to walk back to the shore road and to turn in at the gates of Fernbank. It was strange how much more like coming really home it seemed to be walking into this house in which they had lived for so short a time than it had ever seemed in the house in Cranberry Terrace although they had lived there so many years. Laughter sounded from the living-room, and Joy walked in to find a happy little party gathered round the applewood fire Mr Wrenshaw had insisted upon lighting against the sudden chill of the evening.

Under the light of the electric lamp, Lana looked suddenly more like the lively, lovely girl Joy remembered from the days before her sister's accident had happened. Michael sat beside her, peeling an apple which he handed over to the girl as though laying a trophy at her feet. Impulsively Joy asked: ' What does your father say about all the time you spend with us, Michael?'

There was silence for a moment, then Michael gave a rather forced laugh.

' I'm afraid he doesn't know,' he confessed. ' But he'll have to know one day soon, won't he?' he demanded, looking at Lana.

' That depends,' she answered evasively, Joy thought, but the pretty colour swept into her sister's cheeks as Michael continued.

' I've a B.Sc. in Civil Engineering,' he said without boasting, ' and I can earn a good living in any part of the world. If Father doesn't like what I do, what friends I choose to make, then there's no more to be said. I don't interfere with his life. What right has he to interfere in mine? I'm a man now, not a child.'

' He won't be interfering in mine much longer,' Cara put in. ' I shall soon be living in the Nurses' Home, and I'm over eighteen and shall be earning enough to pay my way, so I'm afraid the days of just moving *me* around like a figure on a chess board to suit his own convenience are over as well.'

'Parents,' Beryl put in unexpectedly, 'can be difficult. But one has to admit it must sometimes be difficult for them too.'

'Granted,' Michael said cheerfully, 'but that's one of the risks I suppose one has to be prepared to take. I mean, there must be lots of compensations to having a family as well as all the obligations and queer bits that come along in the fullness of time! If only parents would realize when it's time to let go of the leading strings, so to speak, and that one is old enough to stand on one's own feet. . . .'

The discussion was waxing fast and furious when Quentin tapped on the door and came in. He looked round at the assembled company, then directly at Joy.

'I just popped in as I passed to let you know your mother's fever has broken and that she's sleeping like a baby,' he told her. 'All she needs now is plenty of rest and quiet, then a week or two resting, relaxing, until she regains her strength. Dad told me when he came in a few minutes ago, and I thought I'd just come down and tell you myself, rather than telephone.'

'Thanks,' Joy said briefly, but her heart, as always, seemed to be playing tricks with Quentin around, and although she echoed Jenny's immediate suggestion that he should stay and take a 'pot luck' supper with them, she wondered dismally how he felt seeing Lana and Michael so engrossed and apparently so happy together.

'Have we time for a little walk along the beach first, Jenny Wren?' Quentin smiled as he put the question. Long ago he had fallen into the family habit of addressing friendly Jenny by the pet name with which they had endowed her. 'I rather wanted to talk to Miss Joy, and it's a lovely night.'

'Half an hour, maybe three-quarters, Doctor, will that do for you?' Jenny asked, and Quentin nodded, turning to Joy as he did so.

'You don't mind, do you?' he asked, and, feeling as though her heart had left her breast and was somehow lodged uncomfortably in her throat, she shook her head.

'I'll just get a headscarf,' she told him. 'There was a wind when I came back from the Mount tonight.'

'The Mount?' Quentin stared at her in astonishment. 'What were you doing there?'

'I went to tell Sam Bainbridge not to bother Mother any more about gaining the possession of Fernbank,' she told him. 'We . . . parted amiably,' she added quickly as she saw Quentin's look of astonishment.

'I have to hand it to you, Joy,' he commented as, without a protest from her, he tucked her hand under his arm and led the way, striding briskly, down to where the shore road ran to the steps which led them on to the sand. 'Let's walk closer to the sea,' he suggested. 'The sand's firmer down there. I used to bring the dogs down here when I was younger, before I went away to medical school. There's something so satisfying about the sea, the stars and a quiet night,' he mused aloud. 'Seems to make all one's problems fade into insignificance.'

'I feel that too.' Joy was recovering her equilibrium which had been so unexpectedly disturbed by Quentin's tucking her hand under his arm. 'Somehow the mere fact that the sea has been there since the beginning of time, going back and forth, rising and falling, seems to have a strangely soothing quality about it. That and the sky above . . . men in the moon and on rockets, walking in space and all the rest of it notwithstanding. It still seems to give such a feeling of peace one feels instinctively there's something . . . infinite . . . watching, looking after all our concerns, if only we'll allow it to do so, and it's an awful help when things get . . . sort of on top of one.'

'They've been rather "on top" of all of us for the last few weeks, haven't they, Joy?' Quentin asked casually, coming to rest near a breakwater and stopping to lean against it. 'But there *are* a few bright spots as well,' he added, 'if only we can look for them.'

'There are,' Joy agreed, suddenly remembering how frightened she had been when she had thought tragedy seemed about to overtake them through her mother. 'I can't tell you what it meant to have that message about Mother this evening.'

'I can imagine,' Quentin said quietly, 'that's why I came instead of telephoning. There are other "bright spots" too, Joy. Haven't you noticed how much better Lana is looking these days?'

'She is,' Joy agreed. How could she have failed to do so? 'She's so much brighter, so much more willing to try and do little things to help, limited though she may be. She's a different girl, thanks to you and Miss Calvin and Hugh Tate. It almost makes me believe you will be right about her altogether, and that she *will* walk again, be able to take part in . . . real living, just as she used to do.'

'She will,' Quentin said confidently. 'I told you in the beginning that she would. How will you feel, Joy, when your mother—as I'm certain she will one day, whatever the outcome about Fernbank—marries Sam Bainbridge? I hope she does, anyway. They'll be good for each other. He needs someone like your mother that he can spoil, show off and be proud of all at the same time. She needs someone like him, someone she can lean on, when the burden gets a little heavy, and it will go on getting heavy until the twins are through! With your mother married to Sam and Lana able to stand on her own feet again, the Wrenshaws and Cousin Emma well able to take care of themselves and of each other, their roof and board assured, how will you feel then, Joy of the all-giving heart, with so many burdens lifted from your shoulders as it were?'

'I hadn't really thought about it,' Joy hedged. 'I . . . I have my job,' she lifted her chin proudly. He mustn't ever think that anyone who accepted responsibility for Lana, even when she could walk and do all the things she had done in the old days, should also automatically assume any form of responsibility for her too! 'I might try for Assistant Matron somewhere in the future,' she offered. 'I've always fancied that when I'd gained enough experience.'

'I see.' He was silent for a few moments then, taking out his cigarette case and lighter, he lit two cigarettes and passed one to her, drawing deeply on the other before he spoke again. 'And what about . . . Pete?' he asked lightly. 'Doesn't he come into your schemes somewhere?'

'Pete?' Joy's laughter this time was quite genuine, and she was relieved to hear that it apparently held none of the hysteria she had been afraid might sound all too clearly in its revealing depths. 'I think it won't be very long before he and Beryl make up their minds to do something about at least getting engaged,' she prophesied, 'and then Sam will have another fit. That will interfere with another of the favourite schemes he and his partner had in mind, I think.'

' "The best-laid schemes of mice and men," ' Quentin quoted with a small laugh. 'Shall we be getting back?' he went on lightly. 'Jenny Wren will have a fit if we overstay her time.'

He was very quiet on their return walk back to the shore road. What was the use? He asked himself the question, but there was no satisfactory answer. Abruptly, almost at the gate he tried again.

'Joy,' he said, halting abruptly and facing her, so that she had to look up at him, 'will you use your imagination just for a moment, please? Will you try and imagine what it would be like if you loved someone very much . . . not your mother, not Lana or anyone in the family . . . a stranger . . . and you saw there was a burden you might help to lighten, just what difference would it make to you in your life? You'd want to do all you could, wouldn't you, to help?'

'I . . . of course.' Joy wondered what he was trying to tell her. Could he be telling her he hoped, before long, to relieve her of the 'burden' that was Lana . . . Lana whom neither she or her mother had ever regarded as anything but a precious charge for whom they would do their best as long as they could?

'You'd want to help, without letting them feel under an obligation of any kind, wouldn't you?' Quentin persisted. 'Just what difference would someone like that make to your life?'

'I don't know,' she said simply. 'I've never even thought about love like that.' He would never know she was lying to him, she told herself fiercely, never know how much she longed to throw herself into his arms and tell him all that was in her heart. 'As I said before, all this . . . Lana, Mother, the twins, Cousin Emma and the Wrenshaws, they're all part of my life. I can't imagine *anything* making any difference to that.'

'Not even if Lana is soon well again?' Quentin persisted.

Joy made a tremendous effort. Whatever he was trying to tell her she knew no other way in which to help him.

'As I said before,' she reminded him with what dignity she could muster when her heart was playing all these foolish tricks, 'I have my profession.'

'Of course,' Quentin agreed, sighing as he took her by the elbow and propelled her up the path. 'And a very noble one too . . . and now I suggest we go and do justice to whatever Mrs Wrenshaw has prepared for what she termed a " pot luck " supper.'

It was obviously no use, he told himself with resignation. Joy was one of the people born into this world to give out to others all their days. He had known she was like that from the first moment of meeting, but he had hoped that once Lana was able to walk again, once her mother had someone else with whom to share the burdens and responsibilities of family life, Joy would feel free to live a life of her own, a life in which she could enjoy herself like any normal girl and plan to make a life of her own as a woman, with the man she loved and who loved her by her side.

He could wait, he told himself, but it might have been so much easier if only he had not promised Lana and Michael he would keep their secret just a little longer. What was it Hugh Tate had said?

'Any time now we can give it a try. She'll do nicely . . .' but somehow, with the polio scare, the illness

156

of Joy's mother and the arrival of Pete and Beryl on the scene, the essential thing, so far as Quentin was concerned, seemed to have disappeared.

'You ought to tell Joy,' Celia had cautioned him. 'She may misunderstand completely why she's been kept in the dark.'

'Lana wants it to be a surprise,' was Quentin's reply. 'And after all, it's her affair, Mother. I promised, because I didn't want her to grow agitated, as she was doing when I mentioned that Joy ought to be told.'

'Well, dear,' Celia sighed, 'you know what's the best thing to do in the circumstances. But your father says that on no account must Mrs Benyon be worried.'

'I know that.' Quentin's smile had been a little grim. 'It seems everyone hasn't to be worried but Joy! No one seems to mind just how much worry *she* gets! That's one of the reasons I'd like to take her out of it all.'

'You couldn't do that,' Celia had said positively. 'She's not the sort of girl to allow anyone to take her away from what she considers to be her obligations. Miss Barnes knew what she was doing when she chose Sister Benyon to take over Fernbank and all that goes with it!'

That was true, Quentin thought as he watched her now. She was helping Jenny as though she herself were paid to do just that, not as if Jenny ought to be waiting on her, as the older woman would have willingly done, but 'sit down for a while, Jenny, and I'll do the dishes. It won't take more than a few minutes, and you've worked hard all day,' Joy was saying with a smile.

Quentin sighed again, signalled to Michael and the two young men each picked up a tea towel and, despite Jenny's protests, began to wipe the crocks, making a game and a race of it, teasing Joy and making Lana laugh. Beryl found herself dismissed to go and make sure Pete's room was aired, and in less time than they could have believed possible, everything, as Eric Wrenshaw suddenly broke his customary silence to observe, was 'ship-shape and Bristol fashion'. The observation, coming as it did from the normally silent old man, caused a diversion, and when he began to tell them stories of 'my navy days' it became so absorbing that before Quentin looked at his watch and reminded Joy she would have to be on duty the following morning, everyone was ready for a second cup of tea!

'And this time you'll leave the pots, and that's *my* orders, Miss Joy,' Jenny commented. 'Though I must say I've enjoyed this evening as I'd never expected to when I first saw your dear mother and the state she was in when Doctor Quentin called.'

'By the time she's home we'll have had lots more evenings like it,' Michael promised as he prepared to tuck his sister and Beryl into his car and deliver them both home. 'We'll all help keep the flag flying, Joy,' he promised. 'And somehow, with you all here, it's such jolly good fun.'

They were gone at last, and Joy went quietly up to bed, first, as she always did, making certain all was well with Lana and Cousin Emma. Unexpectedly Lana reached up her long arms and hugged her sister.

'I'm glad you were sweet to Miss Barnes, Joy,' she whispered. 'I'm glad you're my sister, because you're sweet to everyone, old and young, well or sick. They didn't name you Joy for no reason! That's what you bring wherever you go! I'm sorry I've been such a trial,' she went on, speaking so low that Joy could scarcely hear the words. 'But it won't be for very much longer, just you wait and see.'

'I hope not . . . for your sake, darling,' Joy whispered back, then stooped to kiss the lovely face good-night. But as she climbed the stairs to her own room she felt her heart would break, whether for Quentin who had worked such wonders for Lana and who, given time, would, she was sure, complete the cure in which he himself had such strong faith and who might yet have to stand by and see her give herself to the other man who so obviously adored her too, Michael Bainbridge, and had so much more of this world's goods to offer than had Quentin, or for herself, because her heart was given too, she could not have said.

She only knew that as she crept into bed she breathed a whispered prayer that the peace she had found for a few minutes as she and Quentin walked by the sea might yet come to her and stay . . . a peace which she knew she would only find when her heart was as deeply loved in return by this man whose very name had come to mean so much in her life.

CHAPTER XVII

September proved to be a far more stable, summerlike month than the stormy and tempestuous July and overclouded August had been. The days were warm and golden, and Aileen, slowly recovering her strength, lay out in the garden part of each day at Joy and Quentin's insistence, her pleasure only marred by the sight of the mounting scaffolding and stacks of timber appearing over the top of the hedge.

Sam Bainbridge's name was never mentioned between mother and daughter, but as he continually sent flowers, chocolates, fruit and all manner of unexpected trifles he hoped would please addressed to Aileen, and continued to take her out three or four times each week, Joy knew he had been sincere in his statement that ' she'll be mistress here the very day she says the word ' still stood.

Aileen, her daughter was relieved to note, seemed happier than she had appeared for some time. Occasionally she sang as she went about the house, something she had not done since they had left the house in Cranberry Terrace.

' He must have kept his word . . . somehow I always believed he would, and hasn't mentioned Fernbank to her again, but,' she shivered slightly as another stack of timber was delivered next door, ' I know he'll do all he can to try and make me sell.'

The twins were happily slipping into their routine of the new Technical College, afire with enthusiasm for their plans for the future which now seemed, to their inexperienced eyes, to be almost within their grasp. Pete was equally happily employed by the Vanmouth Trust, and although he said he felt a traitor in working for the company Joy was fighting, she laughed and told him to ' get on with it. I understand from Beryl you're doing fine and that you'll soon have your own office and extra staff and that, it seems, means the first step to being on the board of directors.'

Pete coloured with pleasure but made no comment. He and Beryl, Joy thought, were obviously made for each other and delighted in each other's company. Michael was happy that the girl his father had hoped he would marry and who had, instead, always been a very good friend but nothing more had found someone whom it was obvious she loved with all her generous heart and who in turn loved her with an equal strength.

Only Lana and Quentin remained a puzzle to Sister Benyon, for try as she might, she could see nothing in Lana's relationship with either the doctor or with the son of Sam Bainbridge which would help her to decide which of the two was Lana's favoured suitor.

'The funny thing is that they both appear content with the arrangement, whatever it is,' she thought as she came home one evening to find, as usual, Michael and Lana engrossed in some intricate leatherwork, a handicraft Lana had recently taken up and appeared to enjoy.

Joy had a night off that night, and as she pondered whether she ought to spend the evening washing her hair and then watching television, or to go to the theatre where a London company was staying for a week and putting on a play she had long wanted to see, the telephone rang.

'It's for you, Miss Joy,' Jenny came through having answered the call, beaming all over her good-natured face. 'It's Doctor Quentin, and he seemed in a hurry.'

Obediently Joy picked up the phone, and Quentin's voice, disturbing as ever, reached her ear.

'I've been given a present, Joy,' he said quickly, as though a little unsure—as indeed he was—of her possible reception of his news, 'a box at the theatre for tonight. It's quite an occasion. The two stars are both amongst the leading lights in London, as you know, and Sir Ivor and Lady Manning are to be present this evening . . . part of the play was written in and around Manning Court, it seems. I found out you were off duty. Will you come with me, please? We could make an occasion of it, and neither of us ever seems to have time off for fun . . .?'

161

Joy hesitated just for a moment, then a burst of laughter from Lana and Michael decided her. Evidently neither she nor Quentin would be missed or needed, and impulsively she made up her mind. At least, she told herself as she cradled the telephone lovingly in her fingers, she would have one night, one evening, to remember!

'Thank you for asking me,' she said politely like a little girl. 'I'd love to come!'

'Wonderful!' He sounded as though he really meant it, she thought in amazement. 'Dress up, there's a good girl. We'll have dinner at the Silver Dolphin first and supper there afterwards.'

Joy left the telephone and went slowly up to her own room to change. She took stock of her wardrobe, and for almost the first time in her life she wished with all her heart that she had spent a little more time and money on gathering together even half the quantity of clothes and accessories which Lana possessed in abundance. From below her sister's voice floated up to her, and when she went to see what it was Lana required, it was to be asked why Quentin had telephoned at this hour of the day. It did not take long to explain, and Lana's reaction was most puzzling so far as Joy was concerned.

'Do you a world of good,' she observed. 'What about his surgery and so forth?'

'Doctor Carstairs is standing in for him,' Joy told her. 'The only problem appears to be . . . I haven't anything in which I *can* dress up, not grand enough or too old, anyway.'

'There's a silver lamé dress of mine, hanging in a plastic bag in my wardrobe,' Lana said thoughtfully. 'I've only worn it once, and it's one of those dateless affairs. There are all the trimmings and so on to go with it in the top drawer in the oak dressing table. It should just about fit you. And you're fair. The touches of blue ought to be a bit deeper, but . . .'

Joy began to protest, but Lana would not listen. She insisted instead that Joy went up to change and came down to show her the finished result.

'If there's anything else you'd rather use in its place, do,' she concluded magnanimously. 'Before long I shall scrap that lot and start all over again.'

Joy made no comment beyond thanking her sister. If Lana intended to 'scrap' all her lovely clothes, clothes she had insisted she needed when she had worked for a brief time on her chosen career, then that meant only one thing. She must have made up her mind to favour Michael, Michael who, whether by his own efforts or via his father, would have the money to enable his wife to 'start all over again' with all the expensive trifles Joy knew Lana considered so necessary in a well-dressed woman's wardrobe.

And if that were so, what of Quentin? Quentin who had done so much to restore Lana even so far as she had progressed to this moment, along the highway to health and happiness? And what of Aileen and Sam? How they would react to this unforeseen, at least so far as Sam was concerned, advent of a union between the two families?

'Whatever's worrying you, or whoever it is that's on your mind right at this minute,' Jenny looked up as Joy came through the door on her way to show Lana and Aileen how she looked in her borrowed finery, 'take my advice and forget all about it. Go out and enjoy yourself. Think of the moment, not the past and not the future! Leave all your troubles, your own and anyone else's here, in the linen basket. I'll keep an eye on 'em until you come back. I'll make sure they don't multiply, but for heaven's sake leave 'em! Haven't you learned by this time that half the things folks worry about never happen anyway? And if they do, they seldom turn out to be as bad as we thought they might be!'

'I believe you're right,' Joy agreed unexpectedly, and then, simply because her mirror had told her she was really looking her best, that the well-designed, well-cut dress did unexpected things for her trim figure and that the blue stones of the necklace, earrings and shoulder brooch brought out unsuspected depths in her blue eyes, she laughed aloud. 'I'll take your advice,' she announced, 'and forget all about everything but enjoying the evening.'

It wasn't too hard to do exactly that, she discovered. When he called for her Quentin's eyes told her the mirror had not been in the least deceiving, and she squashed immediately the mental picture of how Lana had looked in precisely the same dress.

Aileen and Sam, it turned out, were also going to the theatre. Sam had already booked two dress circle seats, but Quentin made no suggestion that they should share his box. They had a delightful evening. The meal at the Silver Dolphin was everything Joy would have expected in such a place, and the play was all the reviews claimed it to be, witty, light yet with a story well worth repeating, the acting superb. They saw Sam and Aileen, both evidently enjoying themselves, and during one interval they saw them chatting amiably with another couple, a strikingly dressed woman with a pleasant face and of about Aileen's age, and a tall, shaggy-haired man who appeared to be in the best of moods.

'I ought not to worry about Mother any more,' Joy thought, watching them. 'She's finding her feet in Vanmouth as she never did in all her years at Wilborough. New friends, new work . . . everything,' and that knowledge seemed to help against the feeling of desertion which seemed to have entered her mind unbidden ever since the trouble between herself and Sam Bainbridge had started.

They looked for Aileen and Sam after the show, for Quentin had the idea that it might be a good thing to ask them to share their supper table at the Dolphin and to put forth a suggestion that part of Fernbank, perhaps the attics not used by anyone, could be leased off as offices of administration for the holiday village, and a connecting way discreetly contrived between the hedge.

'At least it might give him ideas as to how the two things could be worked together, your private lives as a family unit and his desire to house his administration separately from the rest of the village, but Sam and Aileen were nowhere to be seen.

' Let's go, then,' Quentin suggested. ' I just thought we might be able to talk things over amicably while he was so obviously in a good mood and enjoying a meal in pleasant surroundings.'

' I still think it would be a mistake to mention it in front of Mother,' Joy persisted, and Quentin said no more, instead he set himself out to be an entertaining and pleasant companion, always making himself remember he was in the company of someone evidently so dedicated to her profession that she had no time in her life or room in her heart for love.

Sam and Aileen, however, had not gone straight home as Joy and Quentin had believed they must have done. They had accepted an invitation from the couple they had met earlier in the theatre, and who, Aileen had been pleasantly surprised to discover, were Sam's partner and his wife, Mr and Mrs Lowe, the parents of Beryl, the girl Aileen felt was now one of their own family circle.

The Lowes had booked a table at the Green Pagoda, the latest Chinese restaurant to be opened in the town, and had invited Aileen and Sam to join them. Sam ordered wine and the quartet were getting along very well, the meal well in progress, when Bill Lowe dropped what turned out later, Aileen decided, to be quite a bombshell.

' Glad we ran into you tonight, Sam,' he said, beaming. ' I have a little something to celebrate, or rather we have,' he beamed on his wife, ' and it's not much fun celebrating alone, is it? I never realized what a mistake it is to plan other folks' lives along the lines you want them to go without consulting them first,' he admitted. ' I will say I've always been a bit dogmatic along those lines, but I've learned a lesson.'

' In what way?' Sam was toying with his glass and not really paying very much attention, but at Bill's next words the glass crashed down on the table and he had sprung to his feet.

' You know how we'd always hoped that one day

your Michael and our Beryl would sort of unite the families?' Bill said, quite calmly and without anticipating any adverse reaction. 'That was all very well, but it seems the young folks have other ideas of their own. Beryl and that young man you have staying at your house,' he glanced at Aileen, 'came along this evening and asked our blessing on their engagement. We couldn't say no. The lad's a financial genius. I've already told him I'll put him up for the board in due course.'

'Lad? What lad?' Sam's face was crimson, and Aileen reached out a detaining hand as she saw his temper rising, but Sam was past caring. 'Michael knows what we'd planned,' he said fiercely. 'What has he to say about all this? Or doesn't he know?'

'He'll know all right,' Mary Lowe smiled at Aileen as though including her in some conspiracy, Aileen thought worriedly. 'Michael's round at Fernbank too, every night, so Pete and Beryl tell us, so I expect he knew this was coming long before we'd any idea.'

'*Michael?* Round at Fernbank?' Sam could scarcely contain himself. 'We'll see about that!' he said so angrily that even Bill looked more than a little taken aback, accustomed as he was to Sam's outbursts of temper when things did not quite go in the manner he thought they should.

'Steady, Sam,' he began warningly, but Sam was past restraint for the moment.

'Steady, is it?' he demanded angrily. 'And where will *that* get me, I'd like to know? There's Cara, off to the hospital to train as a nurse, if you please, and that Ella Wilkinson saying she won't come back unless I get rid of my " foreigners " as she calls the maid and the cook who've been with me just over a year! She says she's not coming back to work as hard as she used to, and I've to get " proper staff ", whatever she means by *that*, before she'll come back as housekeeper again! And now Michael. . . .'

He glared round the table for a moment, then his glance came to rest on Aileen. She was looking white

166

and frightened, just as his first wife used to do when he had what she always referred to as 'one of his brain-storms'. He could not be cross with Aileen or in her presence. She was someone different from any other person he had met in the whole of his life, and her opinion of him mattered more to him than that of any-one else. He would deal with this matter when she was not present, but deal with it he would, and in no uncertain measure.

'I think we ought to be leaving,' he said briefly, help-ing Aileen into her coat. 'Sorry I haven't had a drink with you on that so-called celebration of yours, Bill, but I'll have to see what can be done about it first. Too many of my plans have been upset since Muriel Barnes left Fernbank to Sister Benyon,' he said darkly, but Bill interrupted.

'Pete put out a very good suggestion about the development of the other site down by the pier,' he was beginning, but Sam was in no mood to listen.

'Save it for a board meeting,' he suggested. 'Not the one where you propose this . . . stranger, either! See you in the morning.' And before Aileen and Mary Lowe could, as they had both intended to do, make plans to meet again, he had swept her before him and out of the restaurant into the car.

Aileen was silent. She could think of nothing to say which might be of any help. She knew what it must mean to a man who had enjoyed having all his own way for such a long time to be set at bay by a slip of a girl like Joy, then to have his daughter-housekeeper sud-denly embark on a career of her own, a career such as she had always wanted, where she could be of service to an unknown number of people throughout her working life.

As if that were not enough, she thought as the car drew up at the gates of Fernbank, Beryl was not to marry his son and unite the two business partners and their families as Sam had hoped she would.

'I . . .' she began as she turned to get out of the car, but Sam gave her a grim smile.

'Don't worry, love,' he said with rough gentleness, 'none of this is between you and me. God willing, nothing ever will be. But '—his anger was not gone and there was a glimpse of it in the hand which smote the steering wheel—'I'll have to break my word. I promised your daughter I'd never mention Fernbank to you again, and I'm doing that right now. Tell her, tell her from me,' he said emphatically, 'that I refuse to be flouted at every turn of the wheel,' and before Aileen could think of any words in which to answer him, the engine roared into life and he was gone.

CHAPTER XVIII

When Joy and Quentin returned to Fernbank it was to discover a distressed Aileen had arrived home some three quarters of an hour or so before them. Lana, surprising everyone by her competent direction of affairs, had asked Jenny to brew a pot of strong, sweet tea and tried in vain to persuade her mother to take two of the small tablets Quentin had left her for relief of pain.

' I don't want or need anything,' Aileen insisted again, quite quietly but very firmly when Quentin and Joy tried to persuade her to take them. ' I'm perfectly all right. Sam is the person we should all be worrying about.'

' I'm afraid I can't possibly do that, not right at the moment,' Joy returned. ' I think he has only himself to blame if he makes himself ill by his bad temper. What on earth he means by saying he's being " flouted " goodness only knows. I'm only keeping my word to Miss Barnes, and because it helps all of us to stay here! It's only because he can't bear not to have everything his own way that he goes off like this. A spoiled child has exactly the same reaction.'

' Except that Sam Bainbridge isn't exactly a child,' Quentin muttered, wishing he had his bag with him and could have given Aileen something to calm her nerves. Not that she appeared to be in need of anything, he was bound to admit. For the first time he was seeing the Aileen who had brought up her family unaided, coped with crises of all descriptions without turning a hair, just as she was apparently doing at this moment. ' Where's Michael?' he added, looking round.

' He went off with Pete and Beryl to look at a house they've seen in another part of the town,' Lana told him composedly, ' and he said he was going to have an early night.'

' Maybe just as well, from what your mother says,' Quentin commented, thinking it might give Sam time to cool down a little if he saw nothing of his son that evening. 'This isn't exactly the time to invite more trouble . . . it's a good thing we didn't ask them to join us and listen to your suggestion,' he added to Joy.

'What suggestion?' She looked up from the sandwiches she and Emma, at the latter's suggestion, were compiling to 'fortify' everyone, as Emma phrased it. Emma, Joy often smiled, always flew to food of some description in any family crisis, and she had to admit it often helped. 'Using the attics we've closed up, you mean?' she defined. 'That's done with,' she said firmly. 'I wouldn't give him the right to enter a dog kennel on the premises, even if we had one.'

'That isn't like you, darling,' Aileen protested, but half-heartedly, and Joy's response was the instant smile her mother could always call to her lips, and when she spoke it was in a less indignant tone.

'I know,' she said, but still firmly, 'but that isn't the point. He gave me his word that he wouldn't mention Fernbank to you again, and see what's happened? He sends a message to say " he won't be flouted at every turn of the wheel " . . . well,' she banged down the last of her pile of sandwiches on to those already on the plate and looked defiantly at Aileen, 'this time he's gone too far. I was prepared to compromise, to help if I could. Now I won't budge an inch. He can do what he likes,' she said briefly, 'bring bulldozers and all the rest of his mechanical equipment if he wants to, and I expect he will if he's going to put in that private bathing pool for the village as he says he is, but I won't give way an inch, not an inch!' she repeated firmly, 'upsetting you again like this!'

'You should get angry more often, Joy,' Lana said surprisingly. 'It suits you, doesn't it, Quentin? Look at her colour, and the sparkle in her eyes! Quite a change from the calm, collected Sister we're accustomed to seeing.'

'She always looks attractive,' Quentin said gallantly, 'but I doubt whether her patients would want to see their Sister Benyon with the light of battle in her eyes!

There's a time and a place for everything, Lana, and I quite agree with you, it's high time Joy stopped letting everyone walk over her, use her, and got round to standing up—just a little—for her rights as an individual! After all,' he took a sip of his tea, and it seemed to Joy his eyes were mocking her over the rim of his cup, an idea which would have appalled Quentin had he known what was racing through her mind, ' if you hope to end up as a Matron one day, and that'll be the next step if you get a post as Assistant somewhere, you'll often find yourself doing battle for the rights of your nurses, things you'll want changing and developing and all manner of things! You might as well get used to the idea.'

' Assistant Matron? Matron somewhere? But I thought . . .' Lana was beginning, but Quentin interrupted her so hastily that for a moment Joy wondered what her sister had been about to say which he was so obviously intent upon preventing her from saying.

' All in the lap of the gods, Lana my child,' he said quietly. ' One doesn't talk of these things.'

' But one *does* talk of the Samuel Bainbridges of this world and how one can best help them,' Aileen put in quietly. ' What was this idea of yours you were going to put to him, Joy? Wouldn't you like to tell me about it?'

It did not take long to explain the scheme Joy had thought might help bring a little easement of the situation between Sam Bainbridge and the people of Fernbank, but even though she listened to the end, Aileen shook her head when Joy had finished.

' I'm sorry, pet,' she said sadly, ' but somehow I don't think it would work out half so well as you anticipate. I don't think Sam is really bothered about possessing Fernbank for his staff and so on, not now. He was, in the beginning, and it certainly seemed a good idea, but he's a strange man. The mere idea that you opposed him from the very beginning seems to have made him all the more determined. He isn't accustomed to opposition, you see, not from anyone.'

' He can't force me to sell,' Joy said sadly, ' or I know he would have lost no time in doing so. I know there's nothing he *can* do about it. I went to see Mr Belding the other day,' she confided suddenly. ' I was so disturbed. I didn't want you '—she smiled at Aileen—' to be upset all over again, but he assured me there was nothing Sam Bainbridge could do, no step he could take he hadn't tried when Miss Muriel was alive. That, Mr Belding said, was why she had left the place in my care. It made me feel whatever happened I should . . . sort of keep faith with her.'

' I couldn't agree more, darling,' Aileen smiled back at her daughter. Quentin, watching them, decided she was the least upset of either of them. ' Don't worry about me,' she said firmly. ' I know Sam loves me, wants me to marry him, but he'll have to learn the way to win any woman's heart isn't to trample on those who've already got a claim on her affections. . . .'

She broke off abruptly, and before Joy could make any response as a furious knocking sounded on the front door. Quentin and Pete looked at one another, and Eric Wrenshaw got to his feet.

' I'll go,' he said quietly. ' After all, it's part of my job. Sounds to be someone in trouble.'

They heard him go along the hall, and both young men were not far behind him, while the womenfolk looked at each other, wondering who on earth would come knocking at their door at this hour of the night. They were not left long in suspense. Eric returned in a few moments, with Michael, a strangely dishevelled Michael, following closely on his heels.

' Sorry to come barging back at this hour of the night, Mrs Benyon,' he apologized. ' I know I ought to have gone to one of the hotels in town, but I felt I had to talk to someone who understood. I've had a fearful row with Dad,' he confessed. ' He said I wasn't to come round here any more, and that Cara wasn't to come either, when she gets any free time. He's got to learn we're neither of us children to be told what to do and where to go, not any longer. I've left the firm and everything to do with it. I shall telephone the London firm who were asking for Civil Engineers willing to go to Nigeria, first thing tomorrow morning,' he concluded.

' Have you had anything to eat lately?' Joy was surprised by her sister's calm, practical tone. Usually she thought of Lana as an onlooker at life, or at least an inactive participant. Now she was seeing for herself that there was more of a change in Lana than she had realized. ' I know you didn't have time for any dinner,' Lana went on. ' You told me yourself you worked right through on the new scheme for that specially difficult bridge.'

' I . . . no.' Michael capitulated so abruptly the situation was almost comical. ' I don't think I'd have said half the things I *did* say if I hadn't been so hungry,' he confessed. ' But I'd been along to the kitchen to see what I could coax out of Cook, and found she and the maid had packed their cases and left on the late train. Seems they'd already had words with Father, because he said some unkind things when he told them Ella wouldn't come back and work with them.'

' In his customary tactful fashion, I suppose,' Lana said softly. ' Jenny, have we anything we can give Michael to make a decent meal?'

' There's steak in the fridge,' Jenny offered, ' and some of that tomato soup I made this morning. I can do a few vegetables or some french fried potatoes.'

' The steak will do fine, Jenny, thank you very much,' Michael told her. ' Don't make a fuss. Just a little something will do . . . and a bed for the night, if you'll be so kind. I shall have to go round to the Mount first thing in the morning and collect the rest of my things. I just flung a few odds and ends into the car and . . . came.'

' You did quite right,' Lana told him, ' didn't he, Mother? That's what friends are for, isn't it? To turn to in time of trouble, I mean.'

' We'll do all we can,' Joy was beginning, but she too was looking at Aileen, remembering that the man who was Michael's father was also the man who wanted to marry her mother! ' Where was your father when you left him, Michael?' she asked. ' Was he all alone?'

' I left him in his study,' Michael said briefly. ' He'll

be all right. He often stays there until the small hours of the morning, thinking things out, he says. I must admit he's had some pretty useful ideas during his midnight sessions . . . but I'd like to bet he won't have any flashes of inspiration this time!'

'If you'll all excuse me,' Aileen said suddenly, rising and taking up her bag and other things from the low table where she had been sitting, 'I'll go up and lie down for a little while. Give me those tablets now, will you, Lana, please. I don't want any of you to disturb me. I'll take these and try to get some rest. Things may look better in the morning.'

They watched her go, and as Joy went across and kissed her mother goodnight she felt an unexpected lump in her throat. It wasn't fair, she thought fiercely. Aileen and her second love should be as happy as any youthful lovers, they had everything they could wish for, looking at the matter from a strictly material angle, that was. Why, oh, why did people's emotions have to enter so deeply and so fiercely into the most commonplace things of life, complicating everything for everyone, whether it was their own doing or not?

'I'll look in when I come up, love,' she offered, but Aileen shook her head, smiling so that Joy might be deceived into thinking she was no longer upset.

'I'd rather you didn't disturb me, if you don't mind,' she said with a firmness she had not used since they were children. 'I shall be quite all right.' At the door she turned and spoke to Michael. 'I think you'll be comfortable in the room next to Pete's,' she told him. 'I hope you too think things may be brighter in the morning.'

'I hope so, Mrs Benyon,' Michael said politely. 'Heaven knows I didn't want to quarrel with Dad. We never have before, simply because I've always given in to whatever he's wanted. But this time I just wasn't having any. Nothing short of a miracle is going to make any difference this time, I'm afraid.'

'Then we must hope for a miracle, that's all,' Aileen said quietly. 'Goodnight, everyone.'

She went quickly and quietly upstairs and to her own room, but she put the two tablets safely away, for she had no intention whatsoever of using them. She had plans of her own, and she did not intend any of the family or their friends to interfere.

'I'll make him listen to me,' she told herself as she changed into a warm jersey and skirt and repowdered her nose. She hesitated a moment before applying a fresh coat of lipstick, but the choice of a brighter shade than she normally wore gave her the feeling of having nailed her colours to the mast!

'If it means *we* quarrel too,' she told her reflection, 'at least it's better to happen now than if we decided to marry! It would be too late then to try and convince him he couldn't bully me into doing whatever he wanted, whether it was against my principles or not!'

She crept downstairs, her handbag under her arm. There was a taxi rank at the end of the shore road, and there would not be many other people requiring a cab at this hour of the night. She was right in her assumption. The rank, save for two drivers dozing at the wheels of their cars, was deserted, and in next to no time she was seated in the first one, being driven to the Mount.

The driver was curious. In common with everyone else in Vanmouth he knew this large, somewhat ostentatious house was the home of Mr Samuel Bainbridge, the millionaire, or so gossip had it, who was planning to rebuild the town to suit his own ideas.

'Shall I wait, ma'am?' he asked as he opened the door. 'Don't appear to be anybody at home so far as I can see.'

'Yes, please wait,' Aileen instructed him. 'I'll not be many minutes.'

She went up the wide steps and rang the bell. There was no light to be seen anywhere, but when she tried the door it opened at her touch. For a moment she hesitated, then the taxi-driver was beside her, plainly having watched what had happened and guessed she was distressed.

'I'll come in with you, if you'd like me to, ma'am,'

he told her, and, suddenly afraid, Aileen nodded dumbly, walking into the wide hall and down the first corridor she came to, switching on every available light as she passed the switches.

They found Sam outside the door of his study. Inside the room the light still burned on his desk and on the walls, but it was evident he had been intending to go somewhere . . . maybe, Aileen thought now, in pursuit of his son, when the heart attack brought on no doubt by his own rage had overtaken him.

' Loosen his collar, please,' she directed the man, ' and then switch on all the heating you can find. Get some blankets . . . anything,' and even as he started to obey her instructions she was dialling the number of Fernbank.

CHAPTER XIX

Quentin rose, stretched and yawned, smiling across at Joy, who was beginning to feel rather tired after her unexpected evening of gaiety, the evening which had started so happily and ended with Michael's unexpected entrance. Michael was in his usual place, on the low chair beside Lana's couch, and afterwards Joy wondered if it had been this instinctive placing of himself in the usual position which had prompted Quentin's next words.

'We must do this sort of thing more often, Sister Benyon!' he said teasingly. 'After all, all work and no play isn't good for either Jack or Jill!'

'It *has* been fun,' Joy agreed, accompanying him to the door, which in itself was something unusual, but which he seemed in some undefined way to be waiting for tonight. 'I wish that hadn't happened between Michael and his father, though.'

'It had to come,' Quentin told her, opening the door. 'Sam will have to remember that his children are grown-up people now, with minds and lives of their own, and that they're both intelligent people, and therefore he ought not to expect them to behave like a couple of puppets of which he holds the strings. He wouldn't respect them if they never stood up to him. Great heavens!' he broke off suddenly as he stood out on the top step. 'What on earth's happening? Come round to the back of the house with me, Joy.'

There was no doubt as to what ' that ' was when they reached the back garden of Fernbank. The stacks of timber, some of the chalets and heaven alone knew what else were well ablaze in the half-created holiday village next door.

'Back to the phone,' Quentin directed. 'We must get the fire brigade.'

'What could have happened?' Joy was asking the questions as she hurried beside him and he flung the answers over his shoulder.

'Who knows? Lots of things could have started a conflagration like that, I suppose. That will be for the police, the insurance companies and, I suppose, the fire brigade to decide. Right now . . .'

Before he had time to finish the sentence the telephone shrilled loudly. Quentin was nearest, and he snatched up the receiver, determined to deal as quickly as possible with whoever their caller might be.

'Quentin?' He recognized Aileen's voice, strained though it was. 'It's Mrs Benyon,' she told him. 'I came to the Mount. I felt I *had* to come. It's as well I did. Sam's . . . he's lying on the floor outside the door of his study. He's cold and clammy to touch, and his face is a dreadful grey colour . . . and I don't like the sound of his breathing.'

'Feel in his coat pocket or look on his desk,' Quentin said crisply. 'He carries—or should carry—little glass capsules for these attacks. Break one in a handkerchief and hold it under his nose. He also has some small white tablets. Give him two, and keep him as warm as you can. Loosen his collar and any tight clothing. . . .' He heard her quick whisper that she had complied with what he had said except for the capsules and tablets. 'Good,' he went on cheerfully. 'Don't worry. I'll be along in a few minutes, but when he comes round keep him as quiet as you possibly can, there's a dear.'

'What is it?' Joy asked. 'Who was that? It sounded like Mother's voice from where I'm standing.'

'It was.' Quentin was dialling the emergency service as he spoke. She waited until he had given the details of the address, telephone number and service required, then as he hung up, assured the brigade would be on its way almost before he had time for anything more, he turned to Joy.

'Sam's had a heart attack,' he said briefly. 'He knows he ought not to allow his emotions—particularly his anger—to get the better of him, but don't worry. He'll be all right. Your mother appears to have coped extremely well. If you'll just let Michael know about

178

the fire *and* about his father, I'll be on my way to the Mount to see what I can do for Sam.'

Joy lost no time in complying with Quentin's orders, for orders they were. She went first into the living-room and told the others what had happened, then raced upstairs to hammer on the doors of the two rooms occupied by Pete and Michael. She shouted her information between the two doors, and within minutes the two young men, who had barely had time to start to undress, were downstairs and out in the garden looking at the holocaust over the fence and wall which divided Fernbank from the proposed holiday village.

'It's got a good hold,' Pete muttered. 'It looks as though it's consuming something highly inflammable.'

'That's the stack of creosoted boards,' Michael burst out so suddenly and so loudly that Pete jumped. 'If it gets along that way the next thing's the petrol and diesel stores for the machines and vehicles, then the cabin with Dad's plans and papers. I left them there today . . . I intended to take them home with me and put them in the safe and I forgot.'

He was gone before Pete had realized what he was about to do, and from inside the house they could hear Lana calling at the top of her voice, demanding to be carried out to ' see '.

' We can carry her between us.' Joy glanced at Pete. ' Chair fashion.'

Pete nodded, but he wanted to be active, doing something, anything to help this conflagration from speading. They carried Lana out of doors to where Jenny had already placed a chair, one of the old-fashioned armchairs with high backs and wooden armrests which had been part of Miss Muriel's legacy. Emma, who had stayed to don a warm coat, came out then with a thick travel rug which she tucked round the shivering girl in the chair.

' I'll go and call the twins,' Jenny muttered. ' They'll want to see this . . . it's a sight they'll never see again throughout their lives, I hope.' But she was too late. The twins had heard Joy's call to Pete and Michael and were already glued firmly to the attic windows, resisting

Jenny's entreaties to 'Come down from there! If the fire spreads, or a spark or something catches on Fernbank, you'll both be trapped!'

She went on her way to Aileen's room, opening the door when she received no answer to her knocking, and when she came down, white-faced, to tell Joy her mother was missing, the girl realized for the first time just how much their little family had evidently come to mean to the devoted couple who shared their home.

'Don't be so upset, Jenny.' Joy put her arm round the old woman's bowed shoulders. 'Mother's all right. She telephoned a while ago . . . that was her call, just as we were going to ring the fire brigade. She went to the Mount. It's as well she did. Mr Bainbridge had had a heart attack, and if she hadn't gone . . .'

'That's why the fire's got such a good hold, then?' Jenny muttered, although it was plain she wasn't really thinking about the fire or the holiday village.

'I suppose so,' Joy agreed. 'Come and sit down outside. You can keep an eye on Lana, if you will, and make certain none of the sparks get on to her rug. I'm going to see if I can do anything to help.'

'I don't suppose so.' Jenny listened intently. 'I heard the Vanmouth brigade come along a few minutes ago. That's another one . . . and another . . . I should leave it to the firemen, Miss Joy. It's their job, and they're trained to know what they're doing.'

There didn't appear to be anything much anyone could do. From their vantage point at the attic windows the twins, excited beyond belief, shouted down reports as to what was going on.

'They're playing some special stuff from their hosepipes on to the far corner,' Rex informed them. 'Looks like that foam stuff they use sometimes, like a froth off the top of the washing machine. I expect that's because there's petrol or something there.'

'Where's Michael?' Lana's urgent fingers were pulling at the fringe of her rug, her eyes were wild with fright, and she looked round in a state of such distress that Joy was instantly by her side.

'He's around somewhere, darling,' she said quietly. 'Maybe he's gone to meet Quentin and his father . . . and our mother. She was at the Mount. Mr Bainbridge had worked himself into another heart attack.'

'That was what Michael was afraid of,' Lana said feverishly. 'He's been warned not to get excited, and he seems to spend most of his waking life in just that state.'

'There's Quentin, with Mother and Mr Bainbridge,' she said quickly. 'I must go and find out if there's anything I can do.'

'Where's Michael?' Sam demanded as soon as Joy drew level with them. 'I must see him. I said some dreadful things to him a little while ago.'

'Take it easy, Mr Bainbridge.' Quentin had gone inside and brought out another chair which he placed on the garden almost beside Lana's own. 'Sit down and keep calm, please! There isn't a thing you can do to help. Everything's being handled by the brigades, and they seem to be winning.'

'I want Michael!' Sam reiterated in an angry tone. 'If I don't tell him now that I'm sorry, that I didn't mean half I said, I may never do.'

'You may never have the chance, sir,' Pete said quietly, coming to stand between Sam's chair and that upon which Lana sat, suddenly tense, her arms resting on the wooden arms of the chair. 'He . . . went round there. Said he had to get some plans and papers and things from the cabin.'

'Merciful heaven!' Sam's jaw dropped and Joy took an instinctive step forward, fearing a second attack, but he made a tremendous effort towards self-control, and when he spoke his voice was suddenly that of a very old man. 'If he comes back all right,' he muttered almost to himself, 'he can . . . do as he likes from now on. In fact it might be a good idea to hand my part in the business over to him completely. I'm getting beyond all this sort of thing, and he has plenty of sound ideas of his own, if only he's spared to come back to us.'

Aileen came and stood by the chair. Wordlessly she picked up one of his strong hands as they rested on his knees, but neither of them spoke a word. There was no need of words at that moment. With all her heart she was praying silently that the 'miracle' which Michael had joked about earlier in the evening would really happen, and that when all this was over, Michael would be safe and Sam have learned his lesson without having had to pay too high a price to do so.

'I'm going to have a word with one of the firemen,' Pete said suddenly, close beside them. 'I've got an idea. . . .'

He too was gone, running round to where he had caught sight of the man he recognized as being the mechanic in charge of the fire service vehicles. He had met the man on the day he had brought Joy to her interview at St Lucy's, for Barry Vermont, the fireman in question, had been attending the casualty block, having injured his finger two days before.

'There's a man somewhere in that lot,' Pete jerked his head in the general direction of the hottest and fiercest part of the fire. 'Young Mr Bainbridge. Your folks appear to be getting things under control there, but I was wondering about getting him out. Can you manipulate a crane?' he demanded.

'I manipulate the turntable ladder,' Vermont returned, grinning. 'Don't see there's all that much difference . . . why?'

'There's a crane over there,' Pete pointed, 'a cubic yard effort. They take materials around in it in a thing like a big bucket. I was thinking . . . if we could get it just in front of the cabin . . .'

'I get you,' Barry nodded. 'It's simple . . . but he'll burn his hands on the metal, though there's nothing we can do about that.' He was hurrying as he talked and spoke over his shoulder. 'How did you know it was there?' he queried.

'Because I did an inventory of this site only two days ago,' Pete answered. 'Look, there he is now!'

In the garden of Fernbank everyone was tense with excitement. There seemed little or no danger now of the fire spreading to their own abode, but there still remained the danger of explosion, and already the chief of the brigade had warned them they should seek safety.

'You'll not get much of a blast here, I agree,' he had told them as they demurred, 'but I had to warn you. The risk's your own.'

Lana, sitting erect in her chair, had her gaze riveted to the cabin where so much of importance—at least according to Michael—was kept. She knew there was a small safe, but he had told her often it wasn't 'one would expect Dad to have, not even on a site . . .' and instinct told her that was where he had gone. She tensed in every muscle as she saw him suddenly appear at the scorched and blackened remains of the door of the hut, a dazed look on his face, but the all-important papers and files clasped firmly under his arm.

Deftly Barry swung the big crane round until the huge bucket hovered close to the ground before him. With all her heart Lana willed him to move, to take the few steps forward and to step into the bucket and be lifted to safety.

Quentin, standing with Joy, saw the look on the girl's face as she half lifted herself out of the chair, raising herself by the strong wooden armrests. This was the moment for which he had been waiting, this would show the results of all the patient weeks of persuasion, coaxing and encouragement he had devoted to the sister of the girl he wanted to help more than anything in the world. Gently, careful not to startle Lana, he touched Joy on the arm, and together they watched as Lana, looking exactly as though she were walking in her sleep, rose unaided from the hard supporting chair and took one hesitant step forward.

Beside her Jenny caught back the little cry which sprang to her lips. Joy's fingers, digging into her arm, told the older woman that the miracle she was certain she was witnessing was by no means unhoped-for or unexpected, and she sat silent, her lips moving in word-less prayer, as she watched, along with Joy and Quentin, Lana hold out her arms, standing upright, looking straight at Michael.

He had seen her, and the joy in his face had to be seen to be believed. With his free hand he signalled to the fireman in control of the crane, and, like a majestic prehistoric monster, the bucket was swung high in the air, Michael barely visible inside it, and gently and efficiently lowered into the garden of Fernbank on the other side of the fence.

No one spoke as, with Quentin hovering behind her like a guardian angel, his hands ready to catch her if she fell, Lana made a slow but definite and deliberate progress along the garden until with a sound which was half a sob, half stifled, slightly hysterical laughter, she was caught safely in Michael's arms. He winced as he touched her, the precious papers falling unheeded on the grass.

'I'll take her, Michael,' Quentin told him gently. 'She'll be quite all right now,' and they all knew that he was not simply referring to the events of that night. 'You go with Joy. I've my bag in the car. She'll give you emergency treatment for those hands of yours, then, later, I'll run you up to St Lucy's.'

Sam Bainbridge, in the chair beside the one Lana had so unexpectedly left vacant, looked up at Aileen, and he was not ashamed that anyone should see his eyes were misted with tears.

'He's safe,' he muttered, over and over again. 'I've been given a second chance . . . I'll make it up to him, all the things I said and didn't mean . . . he's always been a good son, and I haven't been fair.'

Aileen smiled. She was wanting to shout her own good news, her own reward of patient, faithful and loving care aloud to a world whether they wanted to hear or not. She wanted to tell them all: 'She walked, Lana walked! She didn't know what she was doing, but she walked . . . it's true what the doctors have said all the time. When she lost Tony she thought she had lost the love of her life, and she didn't want to try . . . she didn't really want to go on. Now she's found a new love, a better love than the old, and it's love that's worked the miracle, love that's given my girl the use of her limbs again, the promise of a new, full life with the man she loves.'

But she said nothing of this, not one word. She took Sam gently by the arm and literally led him into the warm living-room of Fernbank, where Jenny, anticipating Aileen's intention, was already busily laying out cups and saucers, along with a pile of cakes and buns, biscuits and all sorts of things she had baked during the week.

' Eric's got the kettles on, Mrs Benyon,' she looked up from her activities to report. ' I thought maybe the firemen would welcome a cup too.'

' Quite right, Jenny,' Aileen nodded. ' Thank you.'

' You make a better boss than I'll *ever* make, love,' Sam fondled her hand for a moment, his eyes wistful. ' You'll have to teach me not to bully and shout, then people might do things I want them to do without my asking.' He gave a short, hard laugh. ' That is, if you're still willing to try and teach an old dog new tricks?'

' It's never too late to learn, Sam,' Aileen told him lightly. ' Now you just relax, before Quentin has you up in that hospital or a nursing home to make sure you do! I'll be back with you in a moment.'

Left with Jenny, Sam looked at the old woman who had served the people of Fernbank for so many years, and for no reason at all he wished with all his heart that he had accepted Miss Muriel's refusal of his offer to buy Fernbank and not bothered Sister Benyon about it when he discovered the place had been left in her care. He cleared his throat noisily and looked at Jenny from under lowered lids.

' Do you think you could find Sister Benyon and get her to come and have a word with me, while there's no one else about . . . please?' he asked, almost forgetting this was a request and not an order.

' I'll try.' All her life Jenny had distrusted what she thought of as ' sudden changeabouts '. She had never witnessed a successful one yet, she thought scornfully. Look at that Hitler at the time of Munich! Still, everyone seemed to think well of the remainder of the Bainbridge family, and if anyone could reform a character as set in his ways as Sam Bainbridge, then the most likely people to do it were Sister Benyon and her mother. ' I'll see where she is,' she offered, and went out in search of Joy, leaving Sam alone with his thoughts.

CHAPTER XX

Joy was exactly where Jenny had expected to find her. The large back kitchen had been cleared and was being used as a dressing station. Michael, his hands bandaged, leaned back in an old rocking chair with Lana by his side, obviously still shaken both by her own experience and his dicing with death. As Jenny came in Joy emptied the deep enamel basin which she had sterilized and used for a mixture of Milton, warm water and sodium bicarbonate which had been utilized for the making of compresses, then she turned and looked, for once without her customary smile, at the housekeeper.

'What is it, Jenny?' she asked. 'We've just about finished here, and the firemen will all be in for their tea as soon as they've finished whatever it is they're doing outside.'

'It's Mr Bainbridge, Miss Joy.' Jenny sounded disapproving, though she strove to disguise her tone. 'He asked if you'd see him for just a minute, while there's nobody else around.'

'I'll be through in a minute,' Joy told her. 'Whatever it is it will keep until then.'

Jenny left them, and it was very quiet in the kitchen for the next few moments, then, without a word being spoken, but as though each already knew and understood the other's thoughts, Lana and Michael rose, Lana's hand linked through Michael's arm, careful not to touch the bandaged hands.

'We'll go first, Joy,' Lana said quietly. 'We want to tell Michael's father . . . and our mother . . . that we plan to be married, just as soon as it can be arranged.'

'I'm very happy for you both,' Joy said stiffly. She could not look at Quentin, who was busily packing his bag and did not so much as turn his back as Lana made the announcement. He must feel awful, she thought sadly. He had done so much to help, so much to make certain Lana would one day be the bright, happy and whole girl she had been before the accident happened.

'Thanks,' Michael said briefly. 'And thank *you*, Quentin, for everything! I never thought you'd keep our secret right to the end. We didn't anticipate such a spectacular finale, so to speak, but maybe it wouldn't have worked for a long time yet, if fate hadn't taken a hand.'

'Maybe not,' Quentin agreed, still not turning round. 'But I'm glad everything's worked out well for you both. I'll have to keep an eye on those burns . . . and on Lana too, just for a while, but you should both be all right from now onwards.'

They went out, and again silence fell in the kitchen. Joy busied herself about all sorts of little tasks which were by no means imperative or important. She was wondering just what she could say to the man who had just seen the girl he had literally coaxed back to real life walk off and into the arms of someone else, and try as she might there didn't seem any appropriate words which could be said.

Suddenly Quentin snapped his bag closed and took his cigarette case from his pocket, proffering it.

'Well, Sister Benyon,' he began lightly, and although he was smiling she saw that for the first time since she had known him, the smile did not reach his eyes. 'He *is* hurt,' she thought miserably, 'and I don't know how to help him.' He applied the flame of his lighter to the tips of the two cigarettes, looking closely into her eyes as he asked: 'How does it feel to know that one's dream is more or less in one's grasp, as it were? Your mother and Sam will be married before Christmas. So will Lana and Michael. Cousin Emma and the Wrenshaws can manage this place and care for the twins, if we all keep an eye on things. And I heard this morning there's a vacancy for an Assistant Matron coming up next quarter at St Luke's, just a few miles along the coast. Want Father to put a word in for you?'

Joy tried to speak, but couldn't. All at once the words she wanted to say came tumbling out, without her even being aware she was going to utter them.

'I don't care,' she said suddenly. 'I'm not interested, not just at the moment. I can't think about that, not just now. Oh, Quentin, I could see this coming, and I didn't know how to warn you! Lana isn't really mercenary, it isn't just the money, please don't think that . . . she really loves Michael. Anyone watching them when he was swinging in that bucket thing, his face all black with soot and fire smoke, and his hands all blistered, could see for themselves what they meant to each other. It was because of Michael she *walked*!'

'My dear——' Quentin's casual mask was gone and he left his bag, his cigarette burning away unnoticed in the ash tray, and came to take both her hands in his own. 'What are you trying to say to me, Joy?' he asked tenderly. 'Are you trying to tell me that you didn't mean what you said, about going on with your job, wanting to be an Assistant Matron and then a Matron? Is that what you're trying to say?'

'I . . . it was Lana, you see.' Joy was trembling and it took all her courage to meet his gaze bent so earnestly on her own. 'She's so lovely. No man could help but love her. She's beautiful, charming, well read . . . she knows how to talk to everyone. . . .'

'And you know only how to *care* for everyone, to love everyone with that outsize heart of yours, is that it, little Joy?' Quentin asked very close to her hair. 'No wonder I've thought you didn't care,' he murmured, half to himself. 'No wonder I thought you were a career woman, first and foremost. I should have known better.'

'Then you're *not* upset now that Michael and Lana are going to be married?' Joy persisted, and was amazed when he threw back his head and burst into a shout of genuine laughter.

'Upset?' he echoed. 'I'm delighted. It's what I . . . we've worked for all these months, Hugh Tate, Amy Calvin and myself. We knew we could do it, once Lana met Michael and they fell in love. She had an incentive then, to try and make herself do all the things we all knew she could do, that there was nothing really to prevent her doing, nothing except the fact that her own emotional state had prevented her from allowing herself to let her limbs and body function normally, and everything was stiff, unused to co-operating. It took love to work the miracle,' he said softly. ' Do you think it might yet work one for me?'

Joy looked up at him, still bereft of words. It was too much to be true, she must be dreaming, but before she had gathered herself together Sam Bainbridge was at the kitchen door, leaning against the door jamb and looking in on them.

' There's tea poured for the both of you out here,' he told them, ' and a good supper Jenny's knocked together as well. I don't know that I want to talk business in front of everyone there, so I thought I'd better come in here and say what I have to say. You neither of you seem to want to come in and find out what it is. . . .'

' I'm sorry, Mr Bainbridge,' Joy apologized at once. ' We've been a little busy.'

' I can understand that,' Sam growled, suddenly smiling and looking, as Joy said later, almost likeable, ' but will you listen to me for a minute? I'm not going to fight you any more, girl. It wouldn't be worth it, not even after the insurance is paid and everything is settled and done with. I don't want to start on that particular site all over again. But I'm going to marry your mother,' he shot the words at Joy as though issuing a challenge. ' She's agreed,' he told her, ' so I don't think there's any more to be said.'

' Congratulations to you both.' Joy and Quentin said the words almost together, and unexpectedly Sam began to laugh.

' And let's hope I can say the same to you two before the night's ended,' he observed. ' Don't wait until it's too late, or until something happens to make you feel you might lose the one you love, the one who means everything to each of you. . . .'

He turned away and left the door of the kitchen. Wordlessly they looked at one another.

'You kept your promise, Joy,' Quentin said gently, 'you can always be proud of that. Now, would you like to make one to me?'

'I will if I can, Doctor,' she told him, and suddenly her eyes were dancing, and to Quentin she looked more beautiful than the girl who was her sister and the recognized beauty of the family. Here, he thought, was love, devotion, loyalty, all the womanly virtues as well as the beauty of heart, mind and character which enhances the beauties of physical charms and which outlasts them through all the years which lay ahead. Gently he drew her into his arms.

'Give the house to Cousin Emma, Joy,' he suggested. 'You could make it a sort of trust, to be handed on to the twins, one or both of them, when Emma's done with it. I want you to give me another promise, darling, a promise of a very different kind. Sister Benyon'— he put one finger under her chin and tilted her mouth towards his own—'will you promise to love, honour and obey me, till death do us part, so long as we both shall live?' he asked gravely, and the twins, watching unseen but wide eyed through the little side window where they had halted on their way in from the garden, afterwards swore they had caught the faint whisper of Sister Benyon's solemn 'I will.'

PRESENTING...

Harlequin Romances